**Gabe Was ~~...~~
But Nowhere In ~~...~~
Made Allowance ~~... Unplanned~~
Pregnancy. And Now Fatherhood
Was Being Thrust Upon Him.**

And he hadn't even gotten to sleep with the woman.

Not that he wanted to.

Gabe quelled a bitter smile even as his fingers curled into fists, his anger rekindled. Of course he wanted to. But that was a purely physical desire. And physical desires had nothing at all to do with reality. A woman like her did not fit into his plans.

His first priority had to be to get her to trust him. He wanted rights that only she could give him. He would use what little he knew of her to his advantage. And as she began to trust him he would find out what—or how much—she really wanted.

Dear Reader,

Welcome to my second book for Silhouette Desire.

Things and people aren't always what they seem—and that's very much the underlying idea of this book. Chastity Stevens's situation isn't what she at first believes it to be, and Chastity herself is not the woman Gabe Masters thinks he knows.

Throughout the book, Chastity and Gabe are forced to work through their issues (and their attraction), so that by the end of the story, Gabe is the one man able to see beneath the facade Chastity presents to the world, to the woman she is on the inside.

The first glimmer of an idea for this story came when I read a magazine article about a man trying to adopt a child who was biologically, but not legally, his. The circumstances of that case were complex (I think a surrogate was involved), but it gave me the start I needed—that first "what if" question, which for me is often the beginning of a story idea.

I had a lot of fun with the setting of this story, basing Sanctuary Island on a jewel of an island I once stayed on as a parent helper for my daughter's school camp, and adding some convenient alterations of my own.

I do hope you enjoy Gabe and Chastity's story. Please e-mail me at sandra@sandrahyatt.com and let me know what you think.

Sandra Hyatt

SANDRA HYATT

THE MAGNATE'S PREGNANCY PROPOSAL

Published by Silhouette Books

America's Publisher of Contemporary Romance

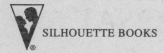

SILHOUETTE BOOKS

ISBN-13: 978-0-373-73004-9

THE MAGNATE'S PREGNANCY PROPOSAL

Recycling programs for this product may not exist in your area.

Visit Silhouette Books at www.eHarlequin.com

Printed in U.S.A.

Books by Sandra Hyatt

Silhouette Desire

Having the Billionaire's Baby #1956
The Magnate's Pregnancy Proposal #1991

SANDRA HYATT

After completing a business degree, traveling and then settling into a career in marketing, Sandra Hyatt was relieved to experience one of life's eureka! moments while on maternity leave—she discovered that writing books, although a lot slower, was just as much fun as reading them.

She knows life doesn't always hand out happy endings and figures that's why books ought to. She loves being along for the journey with her characters as they work around, over and through the obstacles standing in their way.

Sandra has lived in both the U.S. and England and currently lives near the coast in New Zealand with her high school sweetheart and their two children.

You can visit her at www.sandrahyatt.com.

For Wendy, who read everything right from the very beginning, and who was there with friendship (and wine) well before then. You make my world a better place.

One

The boardroom door of Masters' Developments Corporation thudded against the wall. From his seat at the head of the oval table, Gabe Masters looked up sharply to see *her* standing there. Her blue gaze sought and fixed on him. The shock of her sudden appearance registered through every cell of his body. Only years of sitting around this very table, maintaining the bland expression that served him so well in negotiations, kept him in his seat and his shock hidden.

How dare she?

Julia, his PA, appeared breathless at her side. The wildly misnamed Chastity Stevens, with her coiffed honey-blond hair, wearing a figure-hugging black suit as though she was still in mourning, managed to make his elegant PA look downright frumpy. Her perfectly shaped lips were a glossy red, as were her vertigo-inducing shoes and her small elegant bag. Her white-knuckled grip on that bag was the only indication that she wasn't utterly composed.

It was no consolation for her intrusion.

"I'm sorry." Julia shot him a look, her eyes wide. "I couldn't stop her." She reached for Chastity's arm. But with a subtle sidestep, Julia's hand was left flailing in the air.

"It's fine, Julia. I'll handle this." He nodded for his PA to leave.

The gazes of the other men at the table, which had at first flicked to him, were now all fixed on Chastity, noting the porcelain skin, the baby-doll eyes framed by long, dark eyelashes and the seductive curves accentuated by the fitted suit. Curves. He knew just how much those curves had cost. Hadn't his brother, Tom, paid for them, and kept on paying?

Till the day he died.

Gabe fought for composure, fought to keep his voice calm. It was a struggle he'd win. He always did. He stood. "I'm afraid now's not a convenient time, *Ms.*—" he put emphasis on the title "—Stevens." She had never taken Tom's name and he was glad of it. "If you'd like to follow Julia, she'll set up an appointment for you."

"Don't pretend you don't know I've been trying for weeks to make an appointment to see you. It gets old quickly, and infuriating soon after." Her frustration gave Gabe a savage sense of satisfaction. But it wasn't one he could indulge. Not here. Not now.

"I've been a little busy lately." He shared a conspiratorial smile with the men around the table, heard their muted chuckles in response. They'd all been putting in long hours negotiating the purchase terms for his next resort.

That was part of his reason, but he'd also not attached any importance to seeing the gold digger who'd driven a wedge into his family. That damage, now Tom was dead, could never be repaired.

"Excuse me one moment, gentlemen." Gabe strolled toward her. "Leave now," he said in a lethally quiet voice, "and Julia will make an appointment. You have my word." With one hand he held open the door, and with his other gestured for her to leave. She'd made enough of a scene, he needed her gone. A multimillion-dollar deal was at stake here, riding in part on his reputation. It had been difficult enough getting the other men here when so many businesses had wound down for New Zealand's traditional slow, summer month of January.

This deal needed to be signed today. He was not going to have it compromised by her.

He caught her subtle trademark scent of spring flowers—incongruously innocent. What little color had been in her cheeks leached away as she held his gaze for several thudding heartbeats. And even if he'd wanted to, he couldn't have fathomed the expressions that chased one after the other through those wide eyes. Anxiety, he would have said if he'd had to put a name to the predominant emotion. But that made no sense at all. She was the one who'd barged in on his meeting.

Finally, she turned and stepped out of the room.

Gabe nodded to Marco, his second in command, trusting him to take over, before he followed Chastity out.

"You don't seriously expect me to place any faith in your word," she said as he closed the door behind them.

"I don't have time for this. I've asked you to leave. And I meant the building, not just the boardroom." She opened her mouth to speak, but he cut her off. "If you don't, I guarantee you won't get to see me at all, won't get whatever it is you've decided you want from me." He saw her stiffen, saw the flare of delicate nostrils.

Her blue eyes filled with a steely resolve he hadn't seen before. "And if you don't see me right now," she said, "then I guarantee you won't ever get to see the child I'm carrying. Your own flesh and blood."

Gabe could only stare at her as he processed her outrageous claim.

"My office." He spoke through clenched teeth. "Three doors down on the left," he added, though she knew perfectly well where it was. After all, she'd worked here until two years ago, first briefly for him and then for Tom. Till she'd decided that becoming Tom's wife was a far more lucrative position than being his PA.

Chastity, paler than ever, paused outside his office door. Instead of going in, she glanced frantically around, then veered toward the reception area, breaking into a run as she neared it, pushing through the swinging doors and past the trio of poinsettias on the glass coffee table. His last sight of her was with one hand clamped over her mouth as she raced into the women's restroom.

He was waiting, seething, at the doorway when she reappeared a few minutes later, face still pale, but her head held high. A single damp tendril of hair clung to her jaw, the only sign anything was amiss.

She knew better than to look for any sympathy from him as she preceded him into his office. The one time he had asked anything of her—that she not stand between

Tom and his family—she had coolly denied having any influence in the matter. Gabe shut the door behind them, then leaned against it. And waited.

But now that she'd presumably gotten what she wanted, his attention, she seemed reluctant to speak. She lowered herself unsteadily onto one of the leather swivel chairs before his desk, her shapely legs pressed together and angled out to the side, one ankle tucked behind the other. She turned to him, opened her mouth, closed it again and looked toward the window. He followed her gaze. The Auckland sky was a clear, bright blue, but whitecaps dotted the distant harbor and low on the horizon, gray clouds gathered, threatening a storm that might finally break the humidity oppressing the city.

Gabe looked back at Chastity. Moisture beaded at her hairline and her hands were clenched around the armrests of the chair. He expelled a harsh sigh and strode over to the hidden bar on the far side of his office. He poured water into a glass, crossed back and held it toward her. Her gaze flicked up, not quite meeting his, before she stretched out a manicured hand and wordlessly took the glass. Gabe moved away, resumed his position at the door, arms folded against his chest.

Chastity wanted to speak, but couldn't as she fought back another surge of nausea. *Please. Not in front of him.* She'd thought she was beyond caring what he thought.

Apparently not. He was the last person on earth she wanted to humiliate herself in front of.

The Masters family, and Gabe in particular, wouldn't take her news well. He'd thought their connection with her was over. Just as she had.

For the last month she'd been agonizing over how to break the news to him. But day after day, week after week when he hadn't returned her calls, her angst had given way to frustration and then anger. Enough anger that she'd stormed in here determined to fulfill her promise to Tom before any more of the year slipped by. Unfortunately the strength the anger had given her seemed to have vanished with her last hasty trip to the bathroom. She took a sip of water then set the glass down on the edge of his desk.

Last night, before her bedroom mirror, she had rehearsed what she planned to say. She'd thought she had it down pat. Brief, informative and above all emotionless, like the man standing in front of her. And yet here she was, in the understated luxury of his enormous office, unable to get even the first word out.

"What do you want? And make it quick." So, maybe he wasn't emotionless. He despised her. It infused every word he uttered. "I have a meeting to get back to."

She forced herself to speak calmly. "If you'd seen me when I asked, I wouldn't have had to do this."

"And what is *this* precisely?"

She'd known it wouldn't be easy, but she'd forgotten the sheer potency of six foot two of angry man. Chastity drew in a deep breath. "I'm trying to do the right thing." Finally, she looked up and met a gaze as dark as bitter coffee. So similar and yet worlds apart from Tom's.

"As much as that would make a refreshing change, I find it *very* hard to believe."

She couldn't entirely blame Gabe for his cynicism. Tom had used her as an excuse for all but severing contact with his family, initially without her knowledge. And then once she found out, she hadn't protested, she had cared only that her presence gave Tom the space he had said he needed. The fact that the distance suited her, too, was an added benefit.

She looked at Gabe, the high-achieving golden boy of the family. All she had to do was give him her news and then leave. "I'm pregnant." The quiet words fell from her lips.

Before she could continue with her carefully planned explanation of the circumstances, Gabe's gaze dropped to her almost flat abdomen, the slight thickening of her waist concealed by her jacket, and then tracked back up. "Now *that* I can believe."

And just like that, the sustaining anger was back. His brother had been dead for three months, and Gabe was implying that she'd slept with another man. Without conscious thought she launched herself from her chair and drew back her arm. His callous insinuation had brought flooding back the humiliation she had thought she'd left behind her years ago.

Gabe's stance changed, ready, eager to intercept her blow. She didn't know what she'd intended, but as her glare locked on his, she caught herself, lowered her arm and sat back down. She wouldn't give him the satisfaction of having her thrown out and bringing assault charges.

And she couldn't afford to indulge her own satisfaction in having at least tried to wipe the smug superiority from his face.

For long seconds a tension-filled silence electrified the air between them.

"How in the hell do you think you're going to convince anyone that a child of yours has anything to do with me or my family?" He paused, his features sharpened, the panther about to strike a lethal blow. "Tom was sterile."

Chastity stood. She didn't have to take this. She'd told him she was pregnant, like she'd promised. It wasn't her problem that Gabe chose not to believe her. "If you'll step aside, please, I need to leave." She walked toward the door, toward Gabe, who remained unmoving. In a few moments she'd be gone, giving them both what they wanted. If only he'd move. Finally she was one step away from him. Contempt burned in his eyes.

Slowly, he shook his head. "I thought you'd sunk as low as you could go. Clearly I overestimated you." He opened the door wide.

Her nails dug into her palms. She'd made her choices in life and she stood by them. He had no right to judge her. She stepped past him, fixed her gaze on the elevator doors beyond the reception area, and, ignoring the blatantly curious look of the receptionist, headed straight for them.

It wasn't till she stood waiting for the car to reach the top floor that she became aware of someone behind her. She glanced over her shoulder. Gabe stood there, arms folded across his chest, feet planted apart like a bouncer at a night club. He was seeing her off the premises.

The elevator pinged, the doors slid open. Chastity stepped in and turned to face him. Granite Man, Tom had sometimes called his older brother. It wasn't hard to see why. But against her will, she also remembered a time when she'd first worked here, when he had at least always been fair.

But most importantly, she reminded herself, there were

two parts to her promise to Tom and she'd only fulfilled the first. She had vowed to tell Gabe not only that she was pregnant, but also how the baby had been conceived. If she didn't do it now she'd only have to come back.

As the doors started to close, Gabe lowered his arms and turned away. Chastity sucked in a deep breath, put out her hand and the doors stopped. Gabe swung back. "What—"

"Things aren't always what they seem, Gabe. And the world won't always fall into place according to your rigid rules." She held his stony expression. Tension arced between them. "Before he died, Tom and I tried IVF." She spoke quickly, just needing to get the words out. "We used the sperm he banked before his radiation therapy." She lowered her hand, and as the doors closed between them, she had the grim satisfaction of seeing Gabe Masters's smooth, chiseled jaw drop open.

Two

At the ground floor, Chastity stepped out into the building's light-filled atrium and, taking deliberately slow, deep breaths, tried to admire the fountain she'd once found both beautiful and soothing. She stared at the glistening play of water, but in her mind's eye could see only a pair of dark, accusing eyes. It would take more than a fountain to erase that image. She should feel relief that she'd kept her promise to Tom. She could now move on. Instead, she felt only a chilly foreboding.

"Explain it to me again." The deep voice, so close, startled a gasp out of her. She whirled to face Gabe, his gaze deadly serious. He stood between her and the exit.

The hope that fulfilling Tom's wishes meant this was over had been futile. Even hoping for a few days to fortify herself after this afternoon's confrontation had been pointless. Of course he would want more. And he'd want it now. But still she tried to delay the inevitable. "Don't you have a meeting to get back to?"

A muscle jumped in the smooth line of his jaw. "Marco's taken over now. He can handle things for another five minutes." He glanced at his watch before looking back at her, waiting for her response.

"I've said all I need to. We can go back to dealing through our respective lawyers. Just like we have since Tom's death." She stepped around him, focusing on the revolving doors of the exit, on the freedom of the world outside. And yet she knew this would be different.

Death was an end. A baby was a beginning.

Within seconds he was beside her, his long, easy stride effortlessly keeping pace with her hurried steps. They entered a section on the revolving door and she had to slow down to follow its ponderous progression. "I'd like you to explain it properly." Gabe spoke calmly, quietly, but Chastity heard the note of urgency that lay just beneath the surface, felt the tension radiating from him.

Together they stepped into the stifling heat. She knew enough about Gabe to understand that if there was something he really wanted, he allowed nothing to stand in his way.

"There's a bench in the park across the road." He made the remark both a suggestion and a command. Chastity considered her options. Her car was only a block away. She didn't have to do this. The afternoon had been harrowing enough as it was. All she wanted was to go home, get out of the confining suit and the torturous shoes and go for a walk, a very long walk, along the beach. She opened her mouth to refuse him.

"Please?" He spoke before she could, his tone quiet and reasonable.

It wasn't a word that would come easily to him, at least not when addressed to her. "All right. Five minutes." She could hold herself together for that long.

She paused when they got to the park bench over-hung by the branches of an oak tree. Gabe looked at her, then sat first as if conscious that the way he towered over her made her uneasy.

Chastity lowered herself beside him, keeping a careful distance. She drew in a deep, deliberate breath. He still used the same cologne he had when she'd worked for him, a scent that somehow seemed uniquely his, one that in her mind she equated with utter, im-movable, unreasoning strength. It wasn't the scent of a brick wall, but it might as well have been.

She undid the two buttons of her suit jacket. The suit had been fine for his air-conditioned offices; it defi-nitely wasn't ideal for midafternoon heat and humidity, despite the shade of the oak. Dropping her hands to her sides, she ran her palms along the wooden planks of the bench. "I used to sit here sometimes when I worked for you and Tom."

"I know."

She glanced sharply at him, then looked away, watched a team of gardeners weeding a distant flower bed. It made sense. Acutely observant, he was one of those men who seemed to know at all times what was going on with everyone.

"Explain your pregnancy again." Gabe clearly didn't need or want small talk or preliminaries.

It was probably for the best. She could deal in facts

and keep the emotion out of it. He'd angled himself toward her, one elbow resting on the seat back in what she recognized as a deliberate posture of openness. Chastity folded her arms across her chest and watched the gardeners. The sound of their easy laughter carried to her. Their lives surely weren't as carefree as she wanted to believe, but she envied them even the imagined simplicity.

"Tom knew the risk of sterility was high, so before he had his treatment he banked some sperm." Clinical, but she had to be, she couldn't let herself pause or stumble. "Surely you knew that?" Tom's illness had happened several years before she met him. And it was, according to Tom, when he'd still been on good terms with his family and in particular his brother.

Gabe nodded. And waited.

From the corner of her eye, she saw his hands clench into fists. "Several months ago we decided we'd try for a child."

"You went back to the original clinic?"

"Yes. My pregnancy was confirmed a week before Tom's accident."

"He knew?" Gabe's voice was quiet.

She looked up and met the espresso-brown of his gaze, saw the lines that furrowed his brow. Chastity nodded and those lines deepened.

Gabe stood and took a few steps along the path. He lifted a hand to the back of his neck and she heard his muttered curse. She'd never seen Gabe anything other than utterly calm. Never seen him betray that he was as rattled as he clearly was now.

Beyond him tree branches swayed in a gathering

wind that did little to ease the humid oppression of the afternoon. Distant blue-black clouds continued to build on the horizon, threatening, promising, a thunderstorm. A trickle of perspiration ran down between her breasts.

She studied Gabe's back, noted the broad shoulders and the fisted hands now shoved into the pockets of his dark pants. After what felt like an eternity, he turned and walked back to her. His skin had paled and anger and frustration burned in his eyes.

"Thanks to you, Tom all but cut himself off from the family since the day you moved in with him. Why are you telling me this now?"

"Because he asked me to. As soon as the pregnancy was viable, he made me promise that if anything happened to him that I'd tell you about the child, and specifically about how it was conceived." She had agreed only because Tom was finally in excellent health. But excellent health had provided no defense against a rain-slicked road, a sweeping bend and a power pole.

"And what is it you think you want from me?"

"I don't want anything from you. Things can go on just as they have been."

He shook his head. "That's not going to be possible."

"Why on earth not?"

"Because if you're telling the truth, you're carrying a Masters child. And we look after our own."

Chastity stared at him, willing the breath back into lungs that felt like they no longer functioned properly. "*If* I'm telling the truth?"

Gabe lifted one nonchalant shoulder. "You have to admit there are other possibilities."

Chastity stood and started walking. She didn't care where, as long as it was away from him.

She sensed him beside her. "Go away."

"I need the truth."

"As if you'd believe the truth. You only ever believe what you want to hear, see what you want to see."

He kept pace with her.

Unable to shake him off, Chastity stopped and whirled to face him. "All right. The truth is I was never faithful to Tom and I certainly haven't been faithful to his memory. I have no idea who the real father of my baby is, it could be one of dozens of men, so I thought I'd try to convince you it was Tom's, because I'd so like your family's continued involvement in my life. Obviously you're not that easy to fool, so I give up, and now you can go. You won't hear from me again." Her eyes welled with indignant tears and her breath came in shaky gasps.

Gabe didn't move. And neither would she.

He closed his eyes for a moment, opened them again. "I'm sorry if my question hurt you."

His apology was even less expected than his accusation. Gabe Masters never backed down.

Chastity stood frozen.

"We need to talk." With an open palm, he gestured back toward the bench. "Would you rather sit or walk?"

Neither option appealed. As far as she was concerned, she'd kept her promise to Tom. So she should be free of Gabe. "We don't need to talk."

Those searching brown eyes held her immobile. "I need to know what you want, what you're thinking."

"I told you already. All I wanted was to let you

know…the situation. Like Tom asked me. If you or your family want to see the child sometimes as he or she is growing up, we'll work something out."

"My parents will want more than occasional visits at Christmas and birthdays." He paused, then added quietly, "And so will I."

"Really?" She made no effort to hide her surprise or her own cynicism. His family's demands for perfection were what had driven Tom to draw a veil between them and, according to Tom, were what had turned Gabe into a workaholic perfectionist, always striving for bigger and better deals. She'd thought, hoped, they'd be content to carry on pretending she—and by default her child—didn't exist.

"Yes." His conviction was absolute.

A long silence fell before he spoke again. "How are you placed for raising a child?" His gaze swept over her.

"I don't need money, if that's what you're asking." Though quite probably he was questioning whether she had the necessary standards to raise a Masters child rather than the necessary funds.

He nodded once and she wished she knew what was going on behind his serious assessment, because the only thing she could be certain of was that *something* was going on. His brows drew together the way they did when he was working on a problem. And it filled her with foreboding. Gabe Masters didn't make rash decisions. He pondered problems in private and when he'd reached a conclusion, he implemented it. It didn't make him a good team player, but it had made him a phenomenally successful businessman. That, along with a talent for surrounding himself with equally capable and astute colleagues. Most of whom *were* good team players.

Out of nowhere another wave of heat and nausea roiled through her. She looked frantically around but they weren't near the park bathrooms.

Cool hands suddenly framed her face. "Breathe," he instructed, calm and sure. His eyes held hers, calm and sure. With gazes locked, she breathed, slow and controlled, and gradually the nausea, the heat, subsided as though he'd willed it.

"I'm fine now...thanks."

He lowered his hands. She still felt the imprint of his touch, of each long finger against her skin.

She took a small step back. Oh, the indignity of it all. "They call it *morning* sickness. Unfortunately my stomach appears to be synchronized for morning in any number of time zones."

"It's been bad?" He sounded almost concerned.

"Not really. It occasionally ambushes me. It's worse if I'm tired or stressed." Both of which she'd been lately and both because of the prospect of facing Gabe. Now at least that was over. "Look, Gabe. I really need to go. You've had your five minutes."

He glanced at his watch, his frown deepening. "I'll drive you home."

"No." She wanted Gabe seeing and knowing as little as possible about her life. She had her space carved out and it was a comfortable, safe space. It was hers and she got to say who came into it. That list of people was a short one. And Gabe Masters definitely wasn't on it.

"I *am* walking you to your car."

She shrugged. "I don't suppose I can stop you?"

He shook his head. "Not until I'm certain you're okay. And given how pale you are, that's not yet."

They walked in silence. Outside his building he stopped long enough to buy a bottle of ginger ale from a vending machine. "It's good for nausea," he said as he opened it and passed it to her.

Chastity took a grateful sip of the cold beverage, sliding a wary glance in his direction. She didn't quite know how to react to a Gabe who was being...considerate.

She stopped at the small, blue, four-wheel-drive Toyota and beeped it unlocked. Even her car was more of an insight into her life than she wanted Gabe to have.

"What happened to the Mercedes coupe?"

She lifted her chin a fraction. "I traded it."

He clamped his lips together. Ahh, there it was, the familiar cynicism, the slow burn in his dark eyes. As though she had pocketed the cash difference for some nefarious purpose, perhaps a gambling addiction or a drug habit. Chastity showed no reaction. She would be impervious. But it hurt, it always did, no matter how much she pretended to the world, or herself, that it didn't. But that pretense was her only defense. Her armor.

Gabe opened her door for her, closed it as she fastened her seat belt. Finally, with the prospect of escape so close, her tension started to ease. She rolled down her window. His assessing eyes remained steady on her as though searching for something. She turned the key and the engine rumbled into life.

Grim determination settled over the already harsh planes and angles of Gabe's face. His brows drew together. His problem-solving face again. He leaned down, rested his hands on the window frame. "This is not going to work the way you thought it would."

Three

Gabe was only mildly surprised when the doorman called to say he had a visitor, a Ms. Stevens.

After watching Chastity drive away, he had gone back to the negotiation, by which time it was all but signed, and he had let Marco continue to run the show. He'd sat in the room, pretending nothing was out of the ordinary, even commenting a couple of times, nudging things in the right direction when needed. But he was dialing it in.

His thoughts were with her.

With her baby.

With his brother.

As soon as possible after the deal was closed, he'd left. He'd needed time to think, something he did best on his own. So he'd gone to his gym to swim and run and sweat his way through his options till finally he narrowed them down to one.

Then he'd come back to his apartment. It had been little more than an hour since he'd phoned her. He'd known the message he left on her voice mail would get a reaction. He glanced at his watch. He just hadn't expected it to be quite this swift. She hadn't taken any time to consider his offer. He'd purposely phoned late, hoping that she would at least sleep on it and preferably take the weekend before she reacted.

What did surprise him, as he carried his Scotch to the elevator to wait for her ascent, was the curious mix of emotions her pending arrival stirred. The anger and frustration he was used to; it was the charged anticipation that was new. The kind of anticipation he used to feel before going into a negotiation or pulling together a major deal.

It had to be the blond bombshell's bombshell.

In less than a day his carefully ordered life had broken up like a jigsaw puzzle thrown against a wall and he was still determining how best to reassemble it.

He couldn't believe what Tom had done. How he had deceived him. His relationship with his brother, though good in their younger years, had been strained of late. Part of that strain was due to the woman he currently stood waiting for, and the impact she'd had on his family. But if he was honest, there was more to it than just that. Whatever it was, it was far too late to rectify. Tom was gone and he wouldn't be coming back. Ever.

And now there was the child his dead brother's wife was carrying. A complication he would never have foreseen and could still scarcely accept.

On cue the elevator doors slid open. Chastity's blue eyes widened, her chest beneath the white silk of her blouse rose and fell along with her audible intake of breath. She really wasn't any good at hiding her emotions—those eyes were far too expressive.

She was stunningly beautiful. His first sight of her years ago had been like a blow to the solar plexus. It was a reaction he'd learned to manage. He liked a little more substance in his women, something beneath the glossy exterior.

This evening she wore a sleek, black, tailored pant-suit with perilously high-heeled shoes, her face flaw-lessly made up. Had she been out since he'd last seen her, with someone else? Another man? The thought twisted his insides. Despite the aspersions he'd cast on her character earlier, he didn't really want her to live down to them.

"You're looking lovely." He knew she'd hate the blasé compliment, but there'd always been something about her that made him want to upset her composure. "I didn't expect to see you so soon."

"If you'd left me your phone number along with that obscenely ridiculous message, I would have called and saved us both this inconvenience."

She was still so cool, so remote. He'd always sensed there was more going on under the veneer than she allowed the world to see. In that one way they were per-haps similar. "I'll give it to you now," he said, matching her detachment.

"I'm not expecting to need it ever again." Along with the coolness, the steel he'd witnessed in her this after-noon in his boardroom was there again. "Tell me," she continued, "that the *solution* you suggested I consider was just a sick—" her gaze dipped to the Scotch in his hands "—alcohol-fueled joke."

She searched his face and he let her see just how serious he was before he spoke. "I've just poured this. And I don't joke."

"I don't see how it could be anything other. The very idea of you with any baby at all is ludicrous. But to suggest that you—*you*—adopt mine…" She shook her head in disbelief.

He'd been planning to offer money, enough to keep her in luxury for the rest of her life, wondering if despite her earlier assertion, that was what she was truly after. But her vehemence, the righteous anger sparking in her eyes, was more warning than he needed that that offer, at least right now, would be the wrong one to make. Instead he took issue with her use of the word *mine*. "It's not just yours. It takes two to make a baby."

"And this child's father is dead."

Tom. If he were still alive, Gabe might well have throttled him for this stunt. When he didn't say anything further she drew herself up and squared her shoulders.

"You may think—" she jabbed a manicured finger at his chest "—that because you're a Masters, because you were brought up with privilege and you've got money and power, you can do whatever you want. That you can look down your nose at me and push me around till I fall in with your plans." She jabbed again. "Well, I've got news for you, buster. All the money and power in the world doesn't change the fact that this baby is now mine and mine alone."

He caught her surprisingly fragile wrist and drew the jabbing finger away from his chest. His action silenced her words and for a fraction of time they stood there, facing off, inches apart, her hand trapped by his. "It's not money and power that change that fact," he said quietly.

She twisted her hand from his grip. The expression on her pale face tilted up toward him managed to be both mutinous and wary. "What are you talking about?"

Unexpected sympathy for her welled. From this point on, everything she thought she knew would change irrevocably. He probably should have played this differently, prepared her better for what was to come. But then there really was no way to prepare her for it. "Why don't you come in and sit down?" For the first time that he could remember, he was stalling and he wasn't sure whether it was for her sake or his own.

The course of his life was about to change, too. It was up to him to control it.

"No."

He raised an eyebrow. It was a look that had quailed more than one man before.

It had no discernable effect on Chastity. "We have nothing to discuss. I'm only here because I needed you to be very, very clear on that point. And now that I've made it, I expect any and all future communication to be between our lawyers."

Gabe felt a flare of purely objective admiration at her strength and clarity and at the sparks of passion that lit her eyes. A reluctant smile tugged at one corner of his lips. "Tom should have had you as a member of his negotiating team."

"If I need a reference, I'll know where to come." She pivoted on her very high heel.

He'd broken another rule in getting sidetracked from the point at hand. "Wait." She paused at his command, tension in the straight line of her spine, but didn't turn back. "There's something you need to know. Something Tom would want you to know." He tried to make his voice conciliatory.

After several seconds she slowly turned, her gaze wary.

"It's not news you're going to enjoy." That surely qualified as the understatement of the year.

The first fat drops of rain hit the window in his living room. Gabe turned and walked across the marble-tiled entranceway, stepping down into the sunken living room and crossing to stand in front of the floor-to-ceiling window. The raindrops on the glass refracted the light, making the city blur and shimmer in the night. When the full enormity of her—their—situation had first crashed down on him it had stolen the breath from his lungs. An alien and ungovernable tension still hummed within him.

He turned back to see Chastity hesitating at the edge of the tiles, unsure whether to take the next step, or, judging by the way her wide eyes darted from side to side, whether she should run.

"You're here. You may as well listen to what I need to tell you. Besides," he explained as he gestured to the window and the rain that now lashed it, "you don't want to be out driving in that."

If he knew anything about her at all, she probably considered the storm preferable to time with him, but she lifted her chin and took three small steps closer. "What is it you think I need to know?" she asked, skeptical, almost accusatory.

Gabe turned back to the window. He watched her reflection in the glass, saw the defiance in her stance, in the arms folded across her chest as though that could protect her from what he had to say. He met her gaze in the reflection, spoke just loudly enough that he knew she would hear. "The sperm Tom deposited before his radiation therapy was destroyed, by fire, along with almost the entire clinic."

"No." The word was clipped and adamant. She shook her head, her blond hair brushing over her shoulders. "I don't know what game you're playing. Tom and I went back to that very clinic."

"They replaced the clinic. They couldn't replace the... stock."

"No." She was still furiously shaking her head. "Tom told me it was his. 'True blue Masters stock,' he said. He wouldn't lie."

Droplets of water ran down the windowpane like so many tears. "That much is true," Gabe said quietly and saw her confusion.

A flash of lightning split the sky and for a second illuminated the city. "You're contradicting yourself." She spoke quickly, her voice high and tight, discomposed at last and yet he found no satisfaction in it. "You can't even keep your own story straight—a sure sign of lying."

He turned, held her gaze. "I'm not contradicting myself. Tom was only twenty when his sperm was destroyed. He was still recovering physically and emotionally from the cancer and he was devastated." He shrugged. "I wanted to help him. We came up with a solution of sorts." Gabe saw panic building in her eyes. He took a deep breath. "The child you're carrying *is* a Masters. But it's not Tom's child. It's mine."

Chastity didn't know how she did it, but she made it to his couch and sank onto it. "No." She spoke the word quietly this time. Gabe offered no contradiction as he watched her warily, probably wondering whether the cream leather was safe from her rebellious stomach. But there was no nausea, only numb disbelief.

She thought back to her visits to the clinic, to how Tom had been so protective of her, filling in all the forms they needed so all she had to do was sign her name where he had showed her to. And how he had insisted that, should anything happen to him, Gabe know how the child was conceived.

The ultimate deception.

She dropped her head into her hands. And now she was the one paying the price, carrying the child of a man who despised her, who clearly didn't want her as his child's mother. But who did want her child.

She looked up to see that Gabe had turned back to the rain-lashed window and stood motionless in front of it. His hair was slightly disheveled as though he'd run his hands through it more than once.

He didn't joke. He'd said it himself. So hysterical laughter, which would undoubtedly turn into hysterical tears, would be entirely inappropriate. Chastity pushed herself to her feet. Home. She needed to go home. Maybe she'd go to sleep and wake to find this had been just a nightmare.

Her legs were a little unsteady beneath her, but at least the thick carpet muffled her steps. She'd be able to slip out unnoticed. Fixing her gaze on the exit, she took another step. Sudden heat suffused her and the room tilted and started to spin…and then her legs were scooped out from beneath her and she was floating. Disoriented, she pressed her face into the shoulder she was cradled against and for a moment caught that scent of strength and had the fleeting sensation this was indeed all a dream and that everything would be all right.

The sensation passed as she was set back down precisely where she'd been a few seconds ago. The only difference being that now Gabe was at her side and gently guiding her head down between her knees. She lowered her head and tried to breathe calmly, deeply. Thank goodness she was wearing pants rather than a skirt. And now she really did want to laugh. Of all the irrelevant thoughts to have.

Feeling steadier she pushed against the resistance of Gabe's hand and sat up. The hand slid lower, lingered between her shoulder blades and then withdrew altogether.

"Can I get you something to eat or drink?"

"No. I'm fine now, thanks." She tried again to stand. Only to find she didn't even make it to her feet before he grasped her hand and pulled her unceremoniously and, she suspected, effortlessly back down.

"Sit." His tone brooked no argument.

"I'm fine." She tried to inject more conviction into her voice. "Honestly. And I really, really, need to go home."

His grip on her hand stayed firm. "You're not going anywhere yet." He spoke almost kindly, as though it was a fact he regretted as much as he knew she would. "There's a storm outside, you're pregnant, you've had a shock and you just fainted."

There was only one of those four facts that she could even begin to argue with. "I didn't faint."

"If I hadn't caught you, you would have hit the ground."

She'd known it was a weak argument to begin with,

but that didn't make her happy about it. "I've never fainted before."

"Ever been pregnant before?"

"No," she said on a sigh and sagged into the couch. She'd thought she had everything so well sorted out. Well, at least as much as was possible in the circumstances. She was grieving for Tom, but she was financially secure, she had her own house, and if she ever needed anything more—for the baby—she had the shares and other assets she'd inherited when Tom died. An inheritance she'd not even assessed properly yet. But she knew, because Tom's lawyer had told her, that it was substantial.

Finally, Gabe released her hand. "I know how much of a shock this is for you."

She slid her hand in close to her side, away from his touch. "I guess you do." It was probably the only thing about her he really could understand.

Gabe's baby. She was carrying Gabe's baby. Two people who had nothing in common, who wanted nothing to do with each other, were now inextricably bound.

Gabe eased back, as well, and with a barely audible sigh tipped his head back and closed his eyes. Chastity took the opportunity to look at the man who had just turned her world upside down. He shared some of Tom's features, but on Gabe the strong jaw, the dark, straight eyebrows and the liquid brown eyes were somehow different enough to make what on Tom had been charming good looks seem harsher and uncompromising.

Not wanting to get caught studying him, she looked away and surveyed his apartment instead. It was a distraction technique, she knew, but it beat dealing with her current reality. She'd never been here before. Social calls between the two brothers had ended when she had moved in with Tom.

Here again there were similarities and differences with Tom. Both men had a taste for quality but Gabe's was less showy, more masculine. And here at least a person wouldn't have to worry about accidentally knocking over a priceless glass sculpture. Gabe's couch, though cream-colored leather, was deep and soft, the sort you could curl up on with a good book. She thought of her own largely unfurnished home, where she needed to get going to.

"Stay here the night," he said, as if reading her thoughts. And though his words were quiet, they held an implacable ring. He wasn't asking or suggesting. "I have a guest room. Everything's made up."

"No." It seemed to be all she was saying tonight.

"Why not?"

"I can't. I don't want to. And…it wouldn't be right."

"Right?"

"To stay here. In your apartment."

"What are you worried will happen?"

"Nothing. Trust me, I know that. I just don't belong here." *In the home of a man who thinks so little of me.* "I want to go back to my own home." *And bury my head under my blankets to shut the world out.*

"You don't belong out there, either." He gestured to the window as another bolt of lightning split the sky. "At least lie down for a little. You're paler than the couch. Then, when the storm passes, I'll take you home."

She didn't want to admit that he was right, but though she was sometimes stubborn she was generally sensible. "All right. Just for a while," she finally conceded.

He stood and held his hand toward her, but she ignored it as she pushed herself off the couch. She wouldn't let herself need him in any way. It was bad enough that she was giving in to his insistence that she stay. She caught the single raised eyebrow before he turned and motioned for her to precede him in the direction of what had to be the apartment's bedrooms. He kept close, within touching—or catching—distance, as they walked.

"In here." He pushed open a door on their right and Chastity caught her gasp before it escaped her throat. A four-poster bed, piled high with pillows and draped in a lacy white coverlet, dominated the room. To one side sat an old-fashioned armchair and in front of it in the center of a small table, stood a vase overflowing with pale pink tulips. Soft drapes hung at the window.

She walked in and ran her fingers down the closest of the bed's carved wooden posts. It was the kind of room and bed she'd imagined when she'd read fairy tales about princesses late at night in the damp, draughty room she'd shared with her half sisters. Back when her sisters had bothered sleeping at home.

She turned to find Gabe still standing at the entrance, studying her, his expression inscrutable.

"Bathroom's through there." He tilted his head in the direction of an adjoining doorway.

"Thanks." She stepped out of her shoes, and sat on, or rather sank into, the bed. "Am I supposed to be able to feel a pea under this mattress?"

He smiled—actually smiled—straight white teeth showed, the brown eyes crinkled and softened. "It's a little over the top, I know, but I told the decorator this was the one room she could do what she wanted with. It's the only one I never use myself." His smile faded.

"Get some rest. I'll wait up." Was that sympathy, kindness, she heard in his gentler tone?

She considered telling him not to wait up, to get some sleep himself, but that would be like saying she intended to spend the night here. She dropped her gaze to her toes and wriggled them experimentally. At least the shoes hadn't killed them. "Thanks."

She heard the soft click of the door closing.

Reducing the mountain of pillows on her side to one, she stretched out on the bed and closed her eyes. But instead of sinking into the blissful sleep the bed promised, she was assaulted by the recollection of Gabe's information and the implications that would surely have.

Her baby was his baby.

He was her child's father.

And she knew he spoke the absolute truth when he said that visits at Christmas and birthdays were never going to be enough.

Chastity shouldn't have been surprised when sunlight on her face woke her. She'd known she was tired, had known she would sleep—eventually. During the night she had taken off everything but her underwear and slipped between the sheets.

She lay for a moment savoring the big bed, the crisp cotton and the billowy canopy above her. But it was Gabe's bed, even if it was a guest bedroom, and she couldn't help but feel exposed and vulnerable to him here. She rested her hands over the gentle swell of her abdomen. Gabe's bed. Gabe's baby. It was all so very wrong.

She showered quickly, taking just a moment to be impressed by the array of luxury toiletries provided, and had no option but to get dressed in the pantsuit she'd worn last night.

Gabe stood facing the window as she stepped into the living room. Beyond him, sunlight shone on the high-rises of the city and in the distance the harbor sparkled. No trace of last night's storm. He turned. He, too, wore the same clothes as last night. Tiredness lined his face and his dark hair was tousled. A rumpled throw lay on the couch.

"I'm sorry. I slept right through."

He shrugged. "I'd hoped you would."

She didn't quite know how to deal with a Gabe who still sounded concerned for her. It was oddly comforting when really she knew it should make her suspicious. "I thought the pea would keep me awake, but I guess they don't make them like they used to. Or maybe they just make the mattresses better."

His smile was a shadow of the one she'd seen the previous evening.

"And last night, it wasn't just a bad dream, what you told me?"

He shook his head as he walked toward her. No such luck. More like a waking nightmare.

What was he planning? What did he really want? She hadn't forgotten his suggestion that he adopt. He had to have known she wouldn't accept that, but he would likely have a fallback position already planned. Her best move was to get away from here, and him, as quickly as possible.

"By the way," he started quietly.

"Gabe?" The high, cultured voice emanated from the direction of what she guessed to be the kitchen, and filled

Chastity with dread. As if she'd needed another reason to get gone. "I'm sure I left the silver cake knife here after you hosted that soiree before the opera."

"My mother's here," he finished, stating the obvious.

"I'll go." She started to turn, but he grasped her wrist.

"Running won't achieve anything."

She looked up into those serious eyes. "What about hiding? I could survive in that guest room for days. You could slip food under the door."

He shook his head, one side of his mouth tilting up, surprised amusement in his eyes. "Won't achieve anything, either."

"Yes, it will," she hissed. "It'll mean I won't have to face your mother."

"She's going to find out sooner or later. And in my experience sooner is generally better. Everyone can move forward."

"Well, in my experience later, much later, is better. It delays the shouting, the accusations, the pain."

He searched her gaze and then abruptly looked past her.

"Gabe. Why didn't you tell me you had a visitor?" Cynthia's voice carried that falsely bright note that Chastity dreaded.

She turned slowly and watched the older woman's eyes first widen in surprise and then narrow on her. "Good morning, Cynthia." Chastity kept her own voice as even as she could.

"You." Cynthia's gaze dropped to where Gabe's clasp had slid down Chastity's wrist to wrap around her hand. "Gabriel. What's going on?"

Chastity tried to free her hand, but he held firm. He probably thought she'd still try to run.

He'd be right.

"Chastity and I needed to talk last night. She stayed because it got late and because of the storm."

"What could you possibly have to say to that woman?"

Chastity looked at Gabe, imploring him not to tell his mother. Not yet at least. Not while they were in the same room together, preferably not while they were on the same planet.

He gave the smallest nod of his head before turning back to his mother. "Her name's Chastity." His defense surprised her, partly because she was fairly certain that everyone in the family, apart from Tom, referred to her as "that woman."

"My friends call me Chass." She fired one of Cynthia's bright fake smiles back at her, half expecting to hear an angry hissing noise in response. Cynthia, of course, was far too well-bred to make any such noise. But her lips did tighten into an impressively thin line.

"And what is it you needed to talk about?"

Chastity held her breath. After far too long a pause Gabe said calmly, "It was a private conversation."

She squeezed his hand in thanks. He squeezed back before releasing her fingers from his clasp.

Chastity seized her opportunity. "Anyway, I'd like to say it's been lovely seeing you again, Cynthia, but I don't suppose that's been true for either of us. And now I have to go or I'll be late for my…thing that I don't want to be late for." She didn't run, she didn't even walk fast as she made her way to the elevator—but that didn't mean she didn't want to.

A masculine hand reached in front of her to cover the call button. "Can I persuade you to stay and have some breakfast first?" he asked gently.

"I think you know the answer to that one. It goes something along the lines of, *not in a million years*."

He pressed the button for her. "She has another side."

"I'm sure she does."

The doors slid open. Chastity stepped in and turned around. Gabe was studying her, a frown creasing his brow. He tossed something toward her. Reflexively, she caught it. She turned the glossy red apple in her hands. "One bite, deary," she said in a frail, wheedling voice, "and all your dreams will come true."

She looked up to see the raised eyebrow. Oops. "Thanks."

"I'll be in touch."

"I suppose you will."

Making good on his promise, Gabe stood waiting for her in the shadows of a liquidambar tree as she stepped out of the glass-fronted office block where she now worked and into the midday sun. Stunning. Not a hair on her head was out of place. Her lips were the color of ripe plums. A soft cream-colored blouse crossed over her front, revealing a pale vee of skin before hugging her waist. A black skirt clung to her hips, the subtly rounded abdomen, and skimmed her knees. Shapely calves. Slender ankles. Killer heels. And toenails the exact shade of her lipstick.

She was an island of fresh, untouchable beauty in a sea of harried office workers jostling and rushing to make the most of their lunch breaks. Just as he had that morning a week ago in his apartment, he felt the urge to stand between her and the world, or as the case had been then, her and his mother.

Even though she was more than capable of protect-
ing her own interests. Hadn't she proved it with Tom?
Find a rich man, marry him and all your problems are
solved. She was also astute and intelligent. He'd seen
evidence of that in the brief time she'd worked for him.

Before he'd transferred her to Tom's department
because of his attraction to her. An attraction that he
wouldn't allow himself to have for someone who worked
for him. He'd sensed, too, that it was reciprocated.

Or so he'd thought. But after scarcely two months as
Tom's PA, they had come back from a business trip to
Las Vegas and announced their engagement.

His mother placed the blame for the haste squarely
at Chastity's feet.

Gabe had hidden his own quiet fury—at Chastity, at
Tom, but mostly at himself. When the fury ebbed, he
was able to congratulate himself on his lucky escape.

Their engagement had stretched on for eighteen
months, not a day passing that Gabe didn't hope his
brother would see that Chastity wasn't right for him and
call it off. But then one Monday, as Tom sauntered by
his desk at work, he'd thrown out the cocky aside that
he and Chastity had gotten married on the weekend.

She caught sight of him now and he schooled his face
into a neutral expression. He sensed rather than saw her
hesitation. For a moment he thought she might turn. She
didn't. Her step slowed as she approached him. Beneath
her flawless makeup and the impossibly long eyelashes,
he detected a hint of tiredness about her eyes.

Was it her pregnancy that did that, or was it specifically the news that it was his child she carried? News
that had seen him, too, losing sleep.

Gabe was a planner. Yearly, five-yearly, longer term. Backup strategies for if things didn't go as he visualized. He set goals. He achieved them. But nowhere in his plans had he made allowance for an *unplanned* pregnancy. He was always careful. Always. And now fatherhood was being thrust upon him.

And he hadn't even gotten to sleep with the woman.

Not that he wanted to.

Gabe quelled a bitter smile even as his fingers curled into fists, his anger rekindled. Of course he wanted to. But that was a purely physical desire. And physical desires had nothing at all to do with reality, or what was good for him. Or even what was right. A woman like her did not fit into his plans.

Except she had to now. He had to find a way forward.

Chastity didn't look at him, just kept heading down Queen Street, eyes straight ahead. The strange harmony of a week ago, those hours when they had been almost united by their common shock, had gone. He fell into step beside her.

His first priority had to be to get her to trust him. He wanted rights that only she could give him. Today would be the first step in that direction. He would use what little he knew of her to his advantage. And as she began to trust him, he would find out what—or how much— she really wanted.

"You're lunching alone?" His gaze slid over her again as he looked for answers. He only found more questions. Questions he didn't like. Was this woman who carried his child dressed to impress someone at work? He felt the razor-sharp slice of unexpected jealousy. Caused only, he told himself, by the very fact that it was his child she carried.

She said nothing.

He wanted to get under her skin the way she so effort-lessly got under his. "Not meeting a rich, smitten client?" So much for his first priority. Instead of building trust he was antagonizing her, responding to an almost school-boy urge to rile her and ruffle that flawless perfection.

She flicked a glance at him then looked away and quickened her stride, her heels tapping out her frustra-tion at his presence. "If you're done insulting me, you can go." In the instant before her cool dismissal, he'd seen the flash of hurt in her eyes. Was it feigned or real? For someone with such an icy veneer, it shouldn't be so easy to wound her. He expected, needed, her to be tougher, to have an inner hardness that matched the flawless exterior.

She kept walking. Her legs were long, but his were longer and he kept pace effortlessly. "Tom left you enough money?"

"You know he did."

"And as executor of Tom's will, I also know you haven't touched a cent of it yet. Why is that?"

They reached an intersection and she stopped and turned to him, her gaze cool and distant. "Now's not a convenient time to talk."

The lights signaled permission to cross and a crowd of shoppers and workers surged around and past them as they faced each other. She was clearly well aware of the power she held. Her body, her baby. She would be no pushover. He could almost respect that. Almost. He stepped a little closer. She held her ground. "I thought we could have lunch. There's a place nearby. Down at the marina." A light breeze feathered through her blond tresses. And suddenly, as he caught the scent of spring flowers, he regretted the proximity he'd initiated.

Chastity tilted her face up. "Why?" Blatant distrust infused the word and the blue eyes that searched his.

Which was precisely where their problems lay. The distrust was a little rich coming from her. He wasn't the one who'd married someone he didn't love. But he didn't draw attention to that detail. "I want to know the woman who's having my baby."

The words hung in the air between them.

"I can't." Her gaze slid away. "I...uh...don't have long for lunch."

She was a lousy liar. Gabe raised an eyebrow in query and that was all it took for guilty color to climb her cheeks.

Chastity expelled an exasperated sigh. "You know my schedule, don't you?"

He lifted a shoulder. "I like to be in full possession of the facts." He watched her expectantly, curious to see which way she'd jump now. Her wide-eyed gaze met his then tracked away. "Lunch?" he asked again.

The gaze came back, remote and resolute as if she'd called up some reserve of strength. "No." No explanation. No justification or apology.

Gabe didn't think he'd ever been turned down so summarily by a woman before. Clearly she didn't know how much he relished a challenge.

Four

Resisting the temptation to relax and let her guard down, Chastity kept her arms folded across her chest. She turned her face to the sun and wind, felt some of the tension ease that Gabe's presence inevitably caused. She still wasn't quite sure how or why she'd let him talk her into this. She kept most men, most people even, at a distance. That was how she felt safest. But Gabe casually disregarded the barriers she worked so hard to maintain.

He kept challenging her and something told her to challenge right back, that it was imperative to not let him see how deeply he unsettled her.

She chanced a glance at him, standing at the helm, feet spaced wide, hands resting on the large wheel. His suit jacket and tie were lying where he'd tossed them on a seat in the cabin below. The top buttons of his white shirt were undone and the sleeves rolled up. He was missing the eye patch, but with his wind-ruffled hair, broad shoulders and strong tanned forearms, there was a definite air of the pirate about him. Helped by the fact that she felt almost like she was being held hostage. Pirates, she reminded herself, were after treasure. And in this case she knew full well the treasure was not her but the baby she carried. She was not about to let him lay claim to it for himself.

If she wanted him to back off she needed two things. First, she needed him to trust that she would be a good mother and second to understand that she knew what her rights were, and more specifically, she knew what *his* rights were *not*.

"When you said we'd be eating at the marina, I thought you meant at one of the harborside cafés or restaurants."

Gabe looked her way. "Did you?"

"You know I did. So I can only assume that we're on your yacht because a) you don't want to be seen with me, b) you don't want anyone overhearing our conversation, or c) you don't want me to be able to leave whenever I want."

Gabe looked beyond her to the expanse of the ocean. A gull cried out as it wheeled high overhead. "Or d) because I thought you might like it."

"You can have your d) if it makes you feel better, but don't expect me to buy it."

He glanced at her. "It won't make you nauseous, will it? Being on a boat?"

"No," she said honestly, "the breeze helps."

His gaze returned to the horizon. "Tom told me once that you loved the sea. That you'd grown up near it."

"He told you that?" And Gabe had remembered? Of

course he had. He'd have stored the information away in the steel trap of his mind in case one day it came in handy for his own purposes. Like today. Thank goodness she'd never told Tom the full story of where and how she'd grown up. That would only have given Gabe more ammunition, more reason to not want her raising his child.

"It was in the early days."

"Before you stopped talking to each other?"

His brow darkened and she almost regretted having dimmed his obvious pleasure in being on the ocean. From what she knew of Gabe, he didn't do much other than work, devoting his life to the Masterses' empire. Even today he'd taken two phone calls since she first saw him on Queen Street. That he considered their situation worthy of his time and his effort—he'd gone to the trouble of ascertaining the hours she worked—worried her.

His gaze dropped to her. "Can we try starting from this point and moving forward? I won't bring up the past if you don't. At least for this afternoon."

"Does that mean you'll stop insulting me?"

"Yes."

"We could try." She couldn't quite keep the skepticism from her voice.

"Would you rather eat at a restaurant?" he asked, facing her.

"Are you offering?"

"If it would make you more comfortable."

She hadn't expected that and was grateful for it. "No, this'll be fine." She tried to sound conciliatory. The truth was she did love the sea. She had, as he'd said, grown up near it. Not as he might imagine, in a plush beachfront home, but in an isolated, poverty-stricken community, with a family that no one considered upstanding. But the ocean and foreshore had been first her playground and then her sanctuary.

"If it makes you any happier, we're not going far. There's a bay I know that'll be sheltered from this westerly. We'll be there in twenty minutes."

She shrugged her acceptance then turned her focus back to the ocean. It took more of an effort than she would have expected. There was a secret part of her that could have kept watching Gabe and how he handled the boat, how he, too, lifted his face to the sun and wind, just as she liked to. If, as he'd said, this was a beginning and she didn't already know him, she could almost be captivated.

In fact, she had been once.

When she'd worked for him, she'd gotten a secret pleasure from his company, from just being around him. But when she'd inadvertently let her attraction show, he swiftly transferred her to Tom's department. A clear signal that he wasn't interested in someone like her. A man like him wouldn't be. But it had still hurt.

So when Tom made his offer of marriage later, it seemed like a good one. As good as she could expect. Better even.

Lost in thought about choices made, she watched the ocean until they anchored in a small bay surrounded by forested hills. Gabe brought up a hamper from the galley and spread the contents—which looked like they'd been prepared by one of the restaurant chefs— onto the table. They ate in a silence that she wouldn't exactly call companionable but at least it didn't resonate with animosity. Every now and then she caught a glimpse of Gabe, sitting just a couple of feet across from her—his jaw as he chewed, tanned fingers as he tore a bread roll in two.

Finally, Chastity swallowed her last mouthful of sweet strawberry tart and allowed herself to look up and properly meet his gaze. "So, you know about my work?" What else did he know?

"The four mornings a week you work for Knight Architectural? Yes. Jordan told me the week you started."

"Jordan told you?"

His gaze was steady on her. "Seeing as how I regularly send millions of dollars of business his way, it wouldn't pay to do anything to piss me off."

"It always comes down to money, doesn't it?"

"I'm not sure it does with Jordan," he said thoughtfully. "He didn't ask me if he could hire you. He just told me you'd started. He said he thought it was better I hear it from him rather than find out accidentally, as I undoubtedly would."

"You didn't tell him to fire me?"

"Who he employs is his decision."

"And you didn't threaten to pull your business?"

"No. I like the work they do, but I did tell him I didn't want you having anything to do with my account."

"I told him the same thing."

Gabe nodded. "I like to keep business and personal affairs separate." He looked away, lifted his bottle of ginger ale to his lips and took a swallow. There had been a definite insinuation in his statement, a subtle emphasis on the word *I,* an implication that unlike him, *she* did not keep them separate.

Chastity put her fork down. "I didn't set out to snare

Tom, as you and your family believe." Their engagement had been Tom's idea, one she'd given in to in a moment of lonely weakness, but it had turned out to be an arrangement that worked surprisingly well for both of them. Their marriage had been the same. Her two years with Tom had been the happiest of her life and she missed him constantly.

"Of course not."

She ignored his obvious skepticism. The last thing she wanted was to be drawn deeper into a discussion about her relationship with his brother.

"And you and Jordan?" he asked. "I saw the photo of the two of you at last month's gallery opening."

Chastity reeled. She'd just recently buried her husband. And Gabe was all but accusing her of having a relationship with a man who was both her boss and her friend. A man who'd been trying only to cheer her up by insisting she go to the opening. It was that easy to catapult her back to the bleak teenage years when the taunts that were true of her half sisters—and her mother—had also been leveled at her. "So much for refraining from the insults." She pushed her plate away. "It's about now that I'd leave if we were at a restaurant."

"It was a question not an insult. You're remarkably quick to misinterpret."

"Don't blame me. It was an insulting question with an underlying accusation. 'Why would Jordan hire her,'" she mimicked the voices of her tormenters, "'if she's not putting out?'" Chastity cupped her breasts, lifted them up and together, revealing the swell of her cleavage. "'She couldn't possibly have any brains or any skills.'"

Gabe leaned back in his chair. "I'm not apologizing to you because I did *not* say any of those things."

She dropped her hands to the table, clenching them as she leaned toward him, her nails digging into her palms. "Tell me you weren't thinking them."

"I wasn't thinking them," he said quietly. How did he look for so long without blinking, just keeping those brown eyes steady, searching, on her? "I hired you, remember. Not because you *put out,* but because of your brains and your capabilities."

It was Chastity who looked away then. He was right. It had been Gabe who'd first hired her, and he'd expected only that she do her job and do it well. She'd respected him for that. For a time she'd had his respect, too. And the respect of a man like Gabe Masters had meant a lot to her. Which made it all the more painful when she'd lost it.

"I want to know how things stand in your life at the moment, so we can figure out how to move forward," he said.

"You don't need to do any figuring out."

"Yes, I do. This child is mine, too." His dark eyes challenged her.

She met that gaze and played her ace. "Not legally. Sperm donors give up any and all rights." He would know that. He needed to be clear that she knew it, too. Only that fact let her sleep at night.

His jaw clenched and she saw the frustration in his gaze. He'd known all right. "But biologically and morally," he said slowly, "you can't deny that."

Chastity looked over the railing at the water lapping against the side of the boat. Even though the law was on her side, he was right and he'd keep pushing till she acknowledged that. "I'm not denying it, but it means nothing to me."

"Liar." He said the word quietly. "Look me in the eye and say that."

She couldn't. For better or worse—and she was guessing worse—he was her baby's father. That meant something to him. And it meant something to her. Just what that was she still had to figure out. But she had other arguments in her arsenal. "It's a girl," she said.

"Pardon?"

She looked up from the water. "*My*—" she used the word deliberately "—baby is a girl."

A sudden frown marred his brow, drawing his eyebrows together. She was both relieved and disappointed.

"They monitor everything very closely with IVF pregnancies."

If anything, the frown deepened. "You're telling me this because…?"

Suddenly she didn't feel so sure of her ground. His frown wasn't masculine disappointment that would diminish his interest in her child, but anger. Directed at her. "It makes a difference to some people."

"You think…? You seriously think…?" For a moment he was lost for words. "Does it lessen the child's worth to you?"

"No, of course not, but some people…"

He turned away from her, but she'd heard the barely suppressed fury and could see it in the rigid set of his shoulders. And she knew that somehow she'd lowered herself even further in his opinion. The exact opposite of what she was trying to achieve. It was minutes before he turned back to her. "Who?"

She didn't answer, pretended she didn't know what he was referring to, that he hadn't straight away cut to the heart of her assumption.

"What sort of man wouldn't want a child because she was a girl? Other men you've dated?"

"That's not your business. Nor is it relevant."

"Your father?"

"What father?" She snapped the question and the bitterness that tinged those two words surprised her. She never thought about the man who'd fathered her. It must be the pregnancy that had her drawing comparisons, and the contrast with the joy she felt.

Gabe nodded slowly, then spoke through clenched teeth. "I'm not other men." A fact she was well aware of because there was no other man she felt this unsure of herself around.

Gabe pressed a button and the rumble of the anchor chain being drawn up reverberated through the boat.

She'd offended him with her assumption, but given the insults he'd leveled at her, she wasn't going to feel bad about that. Or, at least, she wasn't going to let it show. Because if he sensed any weakness, he'd exploit it.

Gabe stepped back from Chastity's front door and waited. Of course she wasn't home. She would be spending the day with friends, the high-flying crowd she and Tom used to run with, or perhaps family. But not her father.

That she had thought, hoped, that he, too, might ever turn his back on his child had initially angered him. Did she really see him as that inhuman? But yesterday, after he'd walked her to her car in a silence that was far from pleasant, he'd wondered what about her life had taught her to expect others to turn their backs on her? The absent father, of course, but who else? He'd made a mental note to find out more about her, specifically her family. He needed to know what made her tick. Which was why he was here.

He knocked again. This house had surprised him, as far too many things about her were doing lately. He didn't like surprises—they meant he wasn't in full possession of the facts, that he was forced to react.

The weathered cedar home, perched on a remote spot on the craggy west coast, was nothing like the harborside apartment she'd shared with Tom. It wouldn't have been cheap—coastal property never was—and it still had a view of the water, but that was all the two residences had in common. The apartment had been the epitome of inner-city sophistication. Manicured gardens had graced the building's entrance and elegant potted palms dotted the marbled interior lobby. He looked about him. The few trees that had the audacity to establish themselves on the sloping ground here had been punished by the salty wind for it, growing permanently stooped and windswept.

Gabe turned back to his Maserati. The trading of her coupe for the four-wheel-drive made a little more sense. If she was driving the hilly, winding road regularly, she'd need something more practical.

Beneath the distant pounding of the surf, he caught another sound, a quiet clang. He changed direction and made his way around the side of the house.

In a sheltered corner of the garden, a woman with Chastity's face and figure knelt geisha-style on the ground by a small, freshly planted shrub. The impostor's blond hair was pulled carelessly into a high ponytail. She wore knee-length shorts that looked like they'd once—a very long time ago—been a pair of jeans, and a faded red T-shirt. He realized then that he'd only ever seen her dressed in black and white, mainly black. Even before Tom's death. A shovel lay on the ground beside her and she grasped a trowel loosely in her hand, but her gaze was directed toward the pounding white surf and the sparkling blue of the ocean beyond.

She looked fragile and forlorn. A hollowness welled somewhere in the region of his chest. Gabe felt a weakness in his legs that could see him kneeling beside her and an ache in his arms that he could ease by filling them with her.

She swung her head and her eyes widened in her pale face. As she scrambled to her feet, she wiped at her clothes, succeeding only in smearing traces of dirt down her T-shirt. "What are you doing here?" She looked beyond him, checking to see that he'd come alone.

The weakness passed. He made it pass. He was here with the intent of softening her attitude to him, not vice versa. He held up the slim gift-wrapped package in his hand. "A birthday present and a peace offering all in one."

"Oh. Thank you," she said hesitantly. "How did you know?"

"It's the same day as Dad's."

"But," she tilted her head and looked at him suspiciously, "that doesn't explain how you knew it was mine, too."

"It was the reason you and Tom couldn't come for dinner last year, remember?"

She nodded slowly. And though that would ostensibly indicate agreement, he got the feeling she didn't in fact remember and that she wanted nothing more than to send him packing. But she couldn't. Not when he'd brought her a present. Not when she needed him, too, even if she wasn't ready to admit that.

He nodded at the freshly planted shrub. "Interesting way to spend your birthday." He strolled closer. Where were the family and friends he'd envisioned? Why was she here alone?

Chastity followed his gaze and turned back to the shrub as he closed the distance between them, stopping when he stood by her shoulder.

"My cat died yesterday. I planted this for him. It's about the only thing I think will grow here."

"I didn't know you had a cat."

"He wasn't mine really. He came with the house. But he was nice to have around. He helped—" She realized who she was talking to and stopped as she looked abruptly at him. "I'm not even really a cat person." She glanced again at the freshly turned earth. "And I'd only had him a couple of months."

Was she trying to convince him or herself? Because if she could see the tear tracks through the dirt smudges on her face, she'd know she had to work a lot harder before he was even close to being convinced.

"I suppose I should invite you in?"

He should say yes, give her no choice. But he felt like he was intruding here. He shrugged. "Not if you don't want to. I don't want to spoil your day." And maybe it would be better for him, too, if he didn't, if he just turned around and went home and banished the image of a woman alone on her birthday, burying her cat.

She thought for a good long while as he waited, curious to see which way she'd jump, and he worked at persuading himself that it didn't matter to him either way. Sunlight glinted on her earrings which, if he wasn't mistaken, were made of tiny shells and tinsel. A remnant of the recent Christmas? These looked like they'd been made by a child, certainly not a Tiffany's jeweler.

"Hard to spoil it," she finally said with a shrug. "You may as well come in."

Gabe didn't quibble over the fact that the invitation was being extended only because she didn't think even he could make worse what was clearly a lousy birthday. In fact, he felt a surge of relief. Not surprising, he told himself. After all he was here only to establish a rapport with her. He needed her to accept the fact that his name should be on their child's birth certificate, because then he'd have rights. A father's rights. He would do whatever he needed to achieve that. Because whether she liked it or not, he intended to be a significant part of his child's life.

A low timber deck spanned the width of the house, and they crossed the lawn and walked up the two steps that ran along its length. Bifold doors were pushed wide open so that the outdoor area blended seamlessly into the indoors.

The first thing he saw, standing on the kitchen counter, next to a card clearly made by a child, was a black-and-white photo of Tom. In the picture his brother was laughing. It had been a long time since Gabe had seen that particular smile of Tom's. The one that was a combination of joy and mischief, as though he'd just told some shocking but hilarious joke at the dinner table.

Sorrow and regret, for all those things unsaid, the bridges unmended, lanced through him.

He glanced at Chastity, who had stopped by his side. She was looking at him rather than the photo. Her face was turned up to his, her eyes clear, and he read her sorrow, but there was something else there, something that looked like…pity? For him? She broke the gaze. "I'll just clean up." She held aloft her grubby hands between them. "Help yourself to a drink. There's soda in the fridge."

Gabe watched her disappear, followed the sway of her hips, the stride of her long, slender legs. His jaw tightened. Frowning, he turned deliberately and surveyed the room. The almost bare room. His frown deepened. Where was her furniture?

Just like the flow between outdoors and indoors, the open kitchen with its polished hardwood floors blended seamlessly into a dining and living room. Bold, bright, indecipherable artwork hung on the walls and a bookcase brimmed with books stacked two deep. But the dining area held only a small round table with a single chair. And in the living room there was a blue two-seater couch. No TV, no stereo system that he could see. Though in the far corner, incongruous in its ostentation, stood Tom's lacquered, cream-colored grand piano. An affectation because Tom hadn't played. But sheets of music now rested on the stand. Gabe crossed the room, his footsteps echoing in the empty space, and stared at the music—Beethoven—with penciled notations in a neat hand he recognized as Chastity's made in the margins and between the lines of music.

In another corner stood a five-foot-tall piece of

branching driftwood that had been painted silver. Sea-shells, some natural, some painted silver or gold, dangled from the bare branches. Her Christmas tree? Gabe thought of the tree at his parents' house, ten feet tall and professionally decorated, this year's theme colors being silver and blue. He shook his head, not understanding Chastity. And wanting not to want to understand her. Back in the kitchen he found the soda she'd mentioned, and stood looking out at the sea while he drank it.

He turned at the sound of her footsteps and took a few seconds to absorb the blow to the solar plexus. Not only was she fully made up, she'd brushed out her blond hair and now wore a black and white, designer sundress with a fitted bodice and strappy high-heeled sandals. This was an altogether more beautiful woman.

He preferred the other. "What did you do with her?"

"With who?" She tilted her head.

"Your evil twin, or maybe she was the good twin. What cupboard or basement have you locked her up in? I should rescue her."

This Chastity's perfectly painted lips stretched into a smile—a real smile—one that had amusement spar-kling in her clear eyes, one that seemed to make the day itself brighter while it stole some of the oxygen from the room.

He raised his can of soda to her in a toast. "Happy birthday." She looked away from him to face the sea, and he felt the loss of that brief warmth. He hadn't meant to make her smile fade so quickly.

"Thank you," she said quietly.

He closed the distance between them, too aware of

the pale bare shoulder next to him, too aware of the scent of spring flowers. "No family today?"

She tensed. "No." The single word was clipped, a warning to avoid the topic. Nothing fragile or forlorn about this woman. "What about you? Shouldn't you be with your father?" She quickly turned the subject.

"I've just come from the family lunch."

She glanced at his soda. "You'd probably like something stronger then."

He felt a grin tug at his lips.

It had been a predictably awful formal meal, with Tom's absence—the fact that he'd never again be with them—hanging over them. The broken fences would stay that way always. His father usurped Tom's customary role and drank too much; his mother stayed true to form in bitterly and repeatedly pointing it out.

Gabe had been glad to escape, had enjoyed the solitary drive out here. But if his family's day had been marred by Tom's absence, then so must Chastity's have been, and to a far greater extent. As much as he'd doubted that she'd truly loved his brother, or married him for anything other than his money, he hadn't doubted that they'd had a good friendship and an understanding that he had no insight into. Tom had seemed less edgy in the last two years and Gabe attributed that to Chastity's presence. "If I'd known you were alone, I would have invited you."

"To share in the bitterness and accusations, to be treated like something someone stepped in? Gee, thanks."

"We're not that bad."

She didn't answer. She didn't need to. Even today when they'd talked about Tom, his mother, despite

Gabe's corrections, had referred to Chastity, when she'd been unable to avoid it altogether, as That Woman. Maybe being alone really was preferable. It certainly appealed to Gabe. Alone—no responsibility for anyone else's happiness, no bearing the brunt of their bitterness, no tiptoeing around the taboo subjects.

The silence grew heavy, oppressive with memories and, on his part at least, regrets.

"Why are you here?" she finally asked.

"To give you your present." The lie rolled surprisingly easily off his tongue. "I tracked down your address yesterday. You didn't make it easy."

"Maybe because I'm not keen to be found."

"Anyway, I was intrigued."

"Gathering information on the opposition?"

"We're not opposition. We're on the same side."

"Not if you think you have any more rights than an uncle with regard to my child."

He quashed the anger and the arguments that rose. "I didn't want to talk about that today." Not till she was less wary of him.

"Hard to avoid when it's the only reason you're here."

Clearly she hadn't bought the gift reasoning. Smart woman. "Maybe I was worried you were alone."

"And you think your company is preferable to being alone?"

"Good point," he said, unfazed.

She hesitated. "Sorry. That was unkind."

"But true. As far as you know." Funny, she actually looked as though she regretted having said something she thought might hurt him. The remark hadn't even registered on his scale of insults.

"Not entirely. Do you remember the corporate team building? We managed all right then."

The last thing he'd expected was for Chastity to defend him to himself. And with that particular incident.

He remembered too well the session his HR head had convinced him would be a good idea. He had no time for that nebulous touchy-feely sort of thing, but knew that others sometimes got benefit from it. Or so he was told.

So he'd held his tongue and sent his executive team off for several days of making bridges and scaling walls and blindfolding each other or whatever else it was they did on those things. He'd avoided it for the most part, but put in an appearance on the final day.

Chastity, back then his efficient PA, had only been with the company for a couple of months. He was put onto the same team as her, and somehow the two of them ended up spending three hours on a riverbank waiting for their teammates, lost somewhere on the other side, to find the river and build a raft so they could cross and "rescue" them. When he'd accepted it was not going to be a quick process, and ascertained that the quiet, glamorous Chastity was surprisingly relaxed about the whole situation, he'd had no choice but to relax, too. They talked, about nothing in particular, and even told a few corny jokes.

The afternoon had lived for some time in his memory as one of the pleasantest he'd spent in a long while.

When their teammates did eventually turn up with the remains of a raft, it was Gabe and a surprisingly competent Chastity who'd lashed the barrels and bits of wood back together to enable them all to return to shore.

There was no sign of that woman now. He needed to get back something of that rapport. "What are you doing for the next week?" He knew that Knight Architectural practically shut down for the first half of January and that Jordan encouraged all his staff to take their leave then.

"Why do you want to know?" She was guarded, suspicious.

"I'm going to Sanctuary Island to look at the lodge. The deal was finalized just the other day." At the meeting she'd interrupted.

"And?" she asked, her eyes narrowed.

"I want you to come with me."

Those eyes widened with shock and something like fear. "I don't think that's a very good idea."

The fear bothered him. "Because you don't like me?"

She half smiled, but there was no humor in her expression. "Or because you don't like me?"

"I'm trying to like you," he said quietly.

"Against every instinct."

"There's more at stake here than our past…difficulties. Like you said, the team-building exercise, before there was any history, showed us that we can get along." He tried not to think of the night after that afternoon, when they'd all sat around a bonfire talking and singing. Chastity's voice, sweet and crystal clear, had twined inside him, her eyes had glittered in the firelight and he'd been hit with the knowledge that he wanted her.

In a way he most definitely shouldn't.

A few weeks later, when the attraction still hadn't abated, when he thought he'd seen it reciprocated but repressed, he'd had her transferred to Tom's department. And when, a few weeks after that, the desire for her had only grown, he made the decision to ask her out—as soon as she got back from Vegas.

But by then she already had her rich man.

She squared her shoulders and the fear on her face disappeared, replaced by challenge. He couldn't help thinking the bravado was an act. "Face it, Gabe. For once I hold the power. And you don't like it. Admit it."

"I have no problem admitting it. But we have to move forward from here. And you know what's right. That I'm right—about this." He gestured to her abdomen, the slight swelling disguised by the fall of her dress.

She hesitated.

"The lodge isn't finished yet. The original developer went bust on it. There'll be no other guests. You'll have your own chalet right on the edge of the bay. I'll be working. There'll be no pressure."

"You won't try to influence me about the baby, or even talk about it?"

He considered her request. They *would* be talking about the baby. But for that to happen he first had to get her there. "Ultimately we will have to." He gave her that much honesty. "But I won't until you're ready."

"I'll think about it."

Gabe was good at reading people and her *I'll think about it* was a no; she just didn't want to come right out with it. But time was ticking and this was the perfect opportunity. It was a slow period, the first few weeks of the New Year always were. He could use the time to work on her. He'd been considered charming once, back in the days when he'd had to use charm. Of recent years, his wealth and power had been enough to ease the way. He wanted his name on that birth certificate, he wanted rights, because despite what the law said, her child was his. He hadn't planned on being a father anytime soon, but now that he was going to be, he wasn't about to let her cut him out of his child's life.

A young voice called Chastity's name, startling him. Gabe turned in time to see a waif of a girl, all scrawny arms and legs, leap onto the deck and come skidding to a halt just before the door. She straightened, standing tall, pushed her tangled hair back from her face, smoothed her hands down her T-shirt and then stepped gracefully, almost regally through the open door. The transformation reminded him a little of Chastity's. "How was that?" she asked expectantly.

"Beautiful," Chastity said. "Very elegant."

The child beamed and pirouetted. As she spun, she saw Gabe; her Bambi eyes widened and she froze. He half expected her to bolt from the room.

"Sophie, this is Gabe Masters," Chastity spoke quietly. "Gabe, this is Sophie, a friend of mine."

"Hello, Sophie." He wasn't entirely sure of child protocol, but he held out his hand. Sophie, who he guessed to be somewhere around ten or eleven years old, studied his hand. Her gaze darted to Chastity, who gave a small encouraging smile and nodded. Slowly, Sophie extended her hand and shook his. Her fingers were adorned with rings made of shells polished to smoothness by the ocean. A pink shell necklace that rattled faintly as she moved hung around her neck. He felt like he was shaking hands with a sea sprite. "It's a pleasure to meet you, Sophie," he said, smiling.

The girl smiled shyly back.

"I see you have the same beautiful earrings as Chastity."

Sophie touched a hand to her ear and then spun to look at Chastity. "You're wearing them?"

Too late Gabe realized that Chastity would have changed her earrings when she changed her outfit. "She was earlier," he said quickly.

"Of course I'm wearing them." Chastity pushed her hair back behind her ears to reveal her earrings.

"We match," Sophie said, almost breathless. She looked at Gabe as though seeking a witness.

"You do indeed. I feel like the thorn between two roses." He hadn't quite gotten the expression right, but it didn't seem to matter to Sophie who stood taller, her smile widening. Then suddenly recalling herself, she turned back to Chastity.

"Mum wants me to ask if we can borrow a couple of eggs. We've run out."

"Of course."

Chastity crossed to her kitchen and opened the refrigerator.

"She says we'll replace them next Tuesday." The girl looked at the floor. "After Dad's payment comes through. If it's not late again."

"Tell her not to worry. These are from my friend with the farm. She's given me far too many again." Chastity spoke a little too quickly, a little too brightly.

From where Gabe stood, he saw her behind the screen of the open fridge door, transferring eggs from what looked a lot like a store-bought carton into a plastic container.

"Sophie," he said to distract the girl who was craning

her neck to watch Chastity, "I have a friend who used to make her own jewelry from bits and bobs she collected, buttons and glitter and things like that. She now works as a jeweler in London, England. She's designed pieces for movie stars and even royalty."

"Really?"

Gabe nodded. "And it all started with her making things for herself and her friends."

"Really?" she asked again, all breathy excitement.

"Yes, really."

Chastity shut the fridge door and passed the container to Sophie.

"Thanks, Chass." The girl held the eggs to her chest and looked up adoringly at Chastity. "You want to walk on the beach later? I'll show you my cartwheels. I've been practicing."

"Sure." Chastity returned the girl's smile, looking for a moment not that much older than Sophie.

"Great." Sophie headed for the door. "Bye." And then she was gone, running with the eggs clutched under one arm.

He watched Chastity. "'My friends call me Chass?'" That was what she'd said to his mother. And at the time he'd been unable to imagine anyone shortening Ms. Elegant and Sophisticated's name so informally. Not quite so hard to imagine now.

Her smile changed, hinting at a vein of mischief he'd not seen before, and then vanished. "Thank you for distracting her."

Gabe shrugged, still searching her face, her eyes. "She's cute."

"And?"

"And nothing."

"Then why are you looking at me so strangely?"

"Because you keep surprising me. That doesn't happen very often."

"Maybe you shouldn't mix with such boring people." He knew she meant her comment as an insult, a means of distancing them. But Gabe thought of the endless rounds of meetings with architects, accountants and financial controllers that comprised his life lately.

"Maybe you're right." It was her turn to look surprised. About time.

Finally she turned away, busied herself minutely adjusting the position of a fruit bowl on her counter. "Do you really have a friend who's a jeweler who got her start as you said?"

"Yes. I'm not sure about the designing pieces for royalty, but I think she mentioned something like that, and it's entirely possible given what's happening with her career."

"It's so good for Sophie when people recognize her interests and encourage them. To not focus only on how she looks."

That sounded personal. Gabe watched her, curious, but he knew he'd get nothing from her if he probed.

She looked up and he could read nothing in her expression. She was cool and remote. And beautiful. He wanted to strip that practiced neutrality away. He wanted her to smile at him like she'd just smiled at Sophie. He wanted to strip away more than just that, perhaps starting with her sundress. The unbidden thought stilled him. He reminded himself that that wasn't at all what he wanted. He'd written her off the second he'd learned she'd gotten engaged to his brother. "I'll get going, too." Leave, straighten his thoughts out. Maybe that was how she'd snared Tom, by bewitching and confounding him.

She nodded. No argument there.

They walked out onto the deck, and her gaze went to the freshly planted shrub in the corner of the garden.

"Think about the lodge," he said quietly, doing his best to be nonthreatening. "I leave tomorrow and we'll be there for a week. It'd be good if you came. In the meantime, happy birthday again." He picked up the slim parcel from where he had placed it on the outdoor table and handed it to her.

"Thank you." She eyed it dubiously. "You shouldn't have."

He'd never heard a more sincere *you shouldn't have.* "Believe me, it's nothing." And suddenly he didn't want to see her open it. He'd taken too long over the decision of what to get her. He usually delegated gift buying to his PA. In fact, he'd probably even delegated that chore to Chastity in the time she'd worked for him. He hadn't for this gift, despite the fact that Julia was already buying something for his father from him, because he'd been unable to frame the parameters to someone else. *Get something for my dead brother's wife. The woman who's carrying my child. The woman I need to sweeten up.* So, he'd undertaken the job himself. He'd looked in high-end jewelry stores for something tasteful and expensive, but not too personal, nothing that smacked of bribery, although undoubtedly that's what it was. But ultimately he'd ended up buying something that caught his eye on the bargain tables of a bookstore as he'd been striding past. Cheap was touching when it came from a ten-year-old. Not so touching from a millionaire. He should have left it to Julia after all. He mentally shook his head. Way to go, Gabe.

"I'll see myself out."

She nodded, still holding the unopened parcel slightly away from her body, like something distasteful.

Gabe headed slowly, thoughtfully, for his car. Had he played that right? He'd opened his door when she came hurrying around the side of the house, her hair catching the gold of the sinking sun. She drew up, slightly breathless. The book—a journal for recording her thoughts during the weeks and months of her pregnancy—was still clutched in her hand, but now held close to her. He saw its cover, the soft-focus silhouette of a mother cradling her baby that had initially caught his eye.

"Thank you," she said. "This was really thoughtful. I'd thought you might try to do something tacky."

"Tacky?"

"You know what I mean. Try to soften me up with something expensive your PA bought on your behalf, jewelry or whatever. I misjudged you. I'm sorry."

Actually, she'd pegged him just right but she didn't need to know that. He lowered himself into the seat.

"I'll come. To the resort. If that's still all right?"

Victory. He hid the rush that came with it and turned the key in the ignition. "I'll pick you up tomorrow morning."

Five

As the gusts from the helicopter died away and the dark spot in the sky receded, Chastity realized the quick, heavy thumping that continued was her heartbeat and not the rotor blades.

What had she done?

She was on Gabe's territory now and that shifted the balance of power between them.

"What do you think?"

She shot a glance at him, but could read nothing of his expression or intent from behind his dark sunglasses. She knew only that he was watching her, as he had been, subtly, since the moment he picked her up. "That coming here was a mistake."

Her almost overpowering urge was to flee. But she couldn't. Not only because her best means of escape from the island—Gabe's helicopter—had just disappeared from view, but because she needed him to trust her. Trust her enough that he wouldn't make any attempt to fight her for her daughter. If she kept that end in sight, she would get through this.

Besides, she wasn't completely stranded. Here. With him. He'd told her about the arrangements he'd made for the mail ferry that stopped at neighboring islands to also call regularly at Sanctuary Island. But it still felt like being stranded.

One corner of Gabe's mouth stretched into a grin. He, too, was aware of the shift of power. "I meant, of the island? The resort?"

Oh. She turned to look about her. The lodge's buildings were a short stroll away. The largest timber building, with its steep roof and massive windows and a welcoming semicircular entranceway, stood in the open, but other smaller structures—the chalets, she guessed—were nestled in the edge of the forest where it came down to meet gently sloping grass that in turn gave way to white sand. From the beach, a wooden jetty, where the ferry would dock, stretched into the sheltered bay. Water lapped at the shore, and behind her birdsong rang out in the forest. "It's beautiful."

"It is, isn't it?" There was a quiet, awed pride in his voice.

"And not at all what I expected."

"Because it's not like my other resorts?"

"I guess. It doesn't look as much like a playground for the wealthy as the others."

"It's not. This one's a retreat. It's…more personal. I wanted to buy the island from the moment it first came on the market nearly two years ago."

Was Gabe sharing something of himself with her? "Why didn't you?"

"George Tucker wanted it, too. He pushed the price well above what it was worth, and I backed out."

"And?"

"And now Tucker's bankrupt, though not just because of this decision, and I own the lodge he started building."

Or was he subtly warning her? Gabe got what he wanted.

Trouble was she didn't know precisely what he wanted from her, what his agenda in bringing her here was. She knew only that he would have an agenda. And she didn't for a moment believe his claim that he only wanted to get to know her. She still had the message on her answer phone, the one where he suggested he adopt her child. She wasn't about to let herself forget that.

She was trapped in this situation. It wasn't her fault that Tom had tricked them both. If she hadn't been pregnant, Tom's tragic death would have been the end of any contact between them. But—she pressed a hand to her abdomen—she was most definitely pregnant. With Tom's/Gabe's baby.

He wouldn't want the baby for its own sake. She couldn't imagine anyone less likely than workaholic Gabe to want a child in his life. But he wouldn't want Chastity raising his child, either, not when he thought she was nothing more than a gold digger. And not when he blamed her for Tom's estrangement from his family.

"You know with Tom's—your—shares in the company, you're ultimately a part owner of this." His gaze swept the bay and the resort.

She looked again at its quiet beauty. "I hadn't thought of it like that. I don't often—"

"What?"

"Nothing." She didn't think of the shares as hers. She'd use them for her child if she needed, but nothing else.

She reached for the handle of her case, but Gabe beat her to it and hefted it up with a sideways glance at her. He said nothing, but she imagined disapproval in those brown eyes. Disapproval that her case was twice the size and immeasurably heavier than his. She shrugged and walked ahead. "Which way?" she called back over her shoulder.

"Take your pick. Any one of the chalets. They're all mostly finished."

Chastity headed for the one farthest away. Not because she wanted to make Gabe carry her case all that way— that was just an added bonus—but because she wanted her privacy. She'd seen the signs of workmen, scaffolding and ladders against the side of the main building. She wanted to be on her own as much as possible.

"There are no land lines on the island yet," he said as they walked, "but there is cell phone coverage." Chastity nodded.

At the last chalet, Gabe pushed open the door. "And the locks haven't been fitted yet, but it's safe on the island." He looked around the room. "Like I said, it's not completely finished, but it has a bed in it at least."

He waited for her to pass him and enter. She lowered her gaze from the hint of challenge in his dark eyes, but her eyes caught instead on his chest and the dark, button-down shirt that stretched across it, and as she passed him she caught a trace of the cologne that had teased her senses throughout the helicopter flight. She didn't want to be aware of him this way.

But she was.

She fixed her gaze straight ahead. Sunlight shone on a wicker armchair in the far corner of the room. A dresser and a bed with a cream linen coverlet were the only other furnishings. The walls and polished wooden floors were bare.

"I like it," she said. "It's restful."

"Do you mean Spartan?" She heard humor in his voice.

"I mean sparse. But I like sparse. Too many things and I start feeling weighed down."

He hesitated. "But?"

He didn't expand on his question and she knew he was thinking about the apartment she'd shared with Tom. An apartment that overflowed with rugs and furnishings and objets d'art. An apartment she'd been both relieved and pained to leave.

She caught a faint lingering trace of fresh paint—the walls had recently been given a pale mushroom color. "Do all the chalets have beds already?" she asked, changing the subject.

"No."

"Then why does this one?"

"Lucky guess. I called ahead yesterday, told them to make it up. But I wanted you to have the choice. If I'd been wrong it would have been no trouble to change things around."

"Am I that predictable?" She didn't want him to think he knew her. Because he didn't.

"No. This one made sense. It's farthest away from

any construction noise." He lowered her case to the floor. "I'll leave you to get settled in."

But he didn't leave. She waited for him to speak, certain there was something on his mind—probably a warning, or a criticism or an admonishment. But no words came. Finally—finally—when her nerves had stretched to snapping point, his phone rang and he turned and sauntered out to take the call. His crisp, deep voice gradually faded from her hearing.

Chastity ran, her legs pushing through the water. And when the water got too high for her to run, she dove. The ocean closed around her, streaming her hair behind her, cocooning her in cool, muted silence as she swam beneath the surface till the need for air sent her to the top. One breath and she dove under again. Oh, to be a dolphin or a mermaid. Carefree. Being immersed in the water was as close as she could get.

When next she surfaced she swam with strong, easy strokes deeper and farther into the bay. A hundred meters from shore she stopped and looked around the curving shoreline of the small cup-shaped bay. Gabe's bay, despite what he'd said about it being partially hers. What had she done? It was the question that wouldn't leave her alone. A week effectively trapped here with Gabe. A Gabe who could be—and would be, if the day so far was anything to go by—relaxed and charming. Seven days in which she had to be on her guard. Of all the ludicrous ideas. She flipped onto her back and floated.

A dark-haired head broke through the water beside her and she gasped and sank, spluttering, then turned upright and trod water. "Don't do that to me." She pushed wet hair from out of her eyes.

"Me? Don't do this to *you?*" Anger flashed in his dark eyes.

"You startled me."

"What about what you did to me, coming out here alone and then disappearing beneath the water for five minutes?" He was close. Too close.

"It wasn't five minutes and I didn't realize anyone was watching."

"Someone had to watch. You shouldn't swim alone. Fundamental principle of water safety." Droplets of water clung to his dark, spiky eyelashes. She caught sight of broad, slick shoulders, the muscles glistening and shifting as he, too, trod water. She wanted to touch them. She should *not* want to touch them. Beneath the water she made out the indistinct shape of muscular legs working.

"It's a safe beach. I'm a good swimmer." Her foot brushed against his calf and she backed away.

"It doesn't matter how good you are. You shouldn't swim alone." He moved closer again.

Time to set some boundaries. "I may have come to the island with you, but that doesn't give you the right to tell me what I can and can't do." She tried to keep her tone reasonable.

He glared at her. "It's not just you anymore."

The baby. It all came back to that microscopic joining of a part of him with a part of her.

She couldn't bring herself to admit that he might be right this time so she turned from their confrontation and swam toward the pontoon anchored at the northern end of the bay.

Gabe swam beside her.

Chastity strengthened her stroke. She was, as she'd said, a good swimmer. Good enough to get into a U.S. university on a swimming scholarship. Good enough to leave many men in her wake.

But apparently not Gabe.

She swam faster. He kept pace. They were racing hard out as they neared the pontoon. Their hands touched the wooden planks in unison. Her only consolation for not beating him was that he was breathing at least as heavily as her. A couple of seconds later, Gabe surged out of the water and twisted in one lithe movement to sit on the edge of the pontoon, his feet dangling in the water, his shoulders glistening in the sun. That was when Chastity realized her mistake. She would have to sit bare thighed—next to Gabe and hope he didn't notice.

"Come on. I'll help you out." Gabe held his hand toward her. She had no choice. She reached up and grasped it.

"Ready?" She nodded, and in one swift, effortless movement he had her up and sitting beside him, practically touching. She repositioned herself, edging away from his slick, muscled contours, carefully, casually, positioning her hand on the side of her thigh.

"You were right about the good swimmer part," he conceded.

"I know," she said between breaths.

"You competed?"

"For a few years." Swimming had been her way out of the life she'd had, the path to her transformation. The new, improved Chastity.

"Seems like most of the women I've known never swim in anything other than a pool, and even then they never got their hair wet."

Chastity smiled. "I don't know that pushing off from the submerged seat to drift to the far side and order another cocktail really counts as swimming."

"You knew Amber?"

She laughed at his feigned surprise.

Gabe lay back on the damp planking, lacing his fingers behind his head. Her glance caught the curve of his biceps, the pale, softer skin of his inner arms, the contours of defined pecs and toned abs. There was that urge again—the urge to touch. He wore boxers, not swimming trunks. Had he really been that concerned that he'd stripped off his clothes and come in after her? She searched the shoreline and saw a small dark heap that had to be his discarded clothes.

"Thank you," she said quietly, "for your misplaced concern."

She lay down beside him, let the sun warm her skin, and reminded herself who he was. Tom's brother. The man who didn't trust her with her own child. She laid her hands protectively over her abdomen.

White clouds drifted overhead and she heard the faint sound of Gabe's breath next to her ear.

She turned her head to look at him. His face was angled toward hers. She looked into his deep espresso-brown eyes—that's where the danger of sudden drowning lay, and yet she couldn't turn away, couldn't break free of their pull.

She blamed the water, the bay, the sunlight on bare

skin; she blamed pregnancy hormones. She blamed everything she could for the fact that she still wanted, more than ever, to touch him—her fingertips to his jaw, his hair; her lips to his. It was almost a compulsion. The logical part of her brain screamed denials. The blood rushing through her body screamed something else altogether. And she saw his response, a provocation in return.

When and how had this started happening? And what could she do to stop it? The only thoughts she should be having about Gabe were how to get him to trust her. If he guessed what she was thinking, he'd probably try to have her committed. If she didn't beat him to it and check herself in first.

Gabe sat up and his gaze tracked to her thigh. His eyes narrowed.

She glanced at the outside of her leg, saw the pale mismatched patch of skin and sat up, too, positioning her hand over the scar.

"That's what the insurance claim was for?"

As Tom's wife, she'd been covered by the company's medical insurance. And clearly Gabe had seen at least something of her claim from the surgery. "It wasn't for breast implants, if that's what you thought."

Gabe said nothing. His silence and the look on his face told her clearly that was precisely what he'd assumed.

She was tired of fighting him, tired of always putting up a front. "I had a skin cancer removed." She didn't have to tell him, but she wanted to put him in his place. He made far too many assumptions—wrong ones—about her.

His startled expression was at least some compensation. "I'm sorry. Tom never said."

"Why should he? It was none of your business."

"You're right. It wasn't. Isn't. I just figured that you were so...perfect, that it couldn't all be natural."

"Perfect?" It was her turn to frown in disbelief. Gabe thought she was perfect?

"Perfect hair, beautiful face, stunning body," he said dismissively.

"How is it you manage to make what should be a compliment sound like an insult?"

"It's not meant to be either. Just an observation. A statement of fact. You must know it and work at it."

Her looks had been both a curse and a blessing in her life. Chastity looked at their feet dangling in the water.

"You're all right now?" he asked quietly. "The skin cancer?"

She could feel his gaze on her, but didn't look at him. "I'm fine. It wasn't an aggressive type. But they always take out a decent chunk. To be on the safe side."

"I'm glad you're okay." He sounded almost sincere.

She wasn't going to be swayed by it. "So am I."

He reached for her hand, slid it away. She stiffened. She hated people seeing the scar, its ugliness. With a blunt finger he traced the edge of the patch. She tensed even further and grasped his wrist. No one else had ever touched it.

He met her gaze as he drew his hand away. "Does it hurt?"

She released his wrist. "Not exactly. More an uncomfortable sensation."

"I'm sorry. I'd kiss it better if I could."

She gave him her most disbelieving expression before she covered the scar again with her hand. Even Tom had preferred that she keep it hidden.

In a lightning-fast motion he captured her wrist, swept her hand aside, then leaned down and placed his lips over the scar in a quick, searing kiss.

Six

Gabe straightened and Chastity stared dumbfounded at his profile, his relaxed face and posture as he looked out over the water, showing no sign of the shock assailing her. If anything, there was the faintest hint of a smile playing about his lips.

"I like it," he said, aware of her confusion. "Not what it meant for you, but it's so real, so not perfect. So... human."

"You didn't think I was human before?"

"It's difficult to get past the perfection, the reserve."

"Maybe I'm actually shy and that's how it comes across." He wouldn't believe her, but it was the fundamental truth. She usually took a long time to become comfortable with someone, not through want of trying. It's just how she was.

She wasn't surprised when Gabe laughed, though he

cut his mirth short and shot a probing look at her. She didn't want to be the subject of his consideration, didn't want him spending time thinking of her. "So what's the difference?" she asked, needing to distract him.

"Between?"

"Between implants and real? Seeing as how you're such a connoisseur."

"I wouldn't say connoisseur," he said, shaking his head in denial.

"If only I could do the skeptical eyebrow raise."

A smile tugged at his lips. "One or two of the women I've dated…"

"Hmmph."

They lapsed into silence.

"So, what is the difference?"

"I'm not sure that a gentleman would remember."

"No, but you might."

"Seeing as I'm no gentleman." He lifted his hand and a devilish challenge lit his eyes. "Perhaps if I could just…?"

He was teasing and it changed his persona entirely. He didn't seem at all like the Gabe she knew. Hard, uncompromising, unforgiving.

"Not in this lifetime." She, too, kept her tone light. Trouble was, she could almost want his touch. Almost imagine it. That large competent hand… She banished the thought.

The silence returned. His hand lay flat on the wood between them, almost touching her own, with its pink, carefully manicured nails.

"Your fingernails?"

"Mine," she sighed, flicking his thigh in irritation.

He trapped her hand beneath his. "And…your hair? You're a real blonde?"

It was time to put a stop to this before he beguiled her, made her laugh, made her forget completely who she was and, more importantly, who she was with. She slid her hand from under his, turned to him, went for her haughtiest expression. "You'll never know."

The look was one that years ago she'd worked on in front of the mirror as she was sloughing off the old Chastity, the Chastity who was frightened and uncertain and far too easily intimidated. It was a deliberately frosty expression that saw most men back off. It didn't work on Gabe. Clearly, he wasn't most men. The barest hint of a smile registered on his full lips and his stare lingered and heated. "Is that a challenge?" And Chastity was certain her own body temperature rose with it.

"Just a statement of fact." She tried to be as coolly dismissive as he had earlier, but given the masculine appraisal in his dark eyes, he wasn't going to be that easy to dismiss. She'd forgotten how competitive Gabe was, how he took on any challenge he thought he could win—and won. She wasn't going to get into any kind of power play with him.

Pushing off with her hands, she slipped into the water, let it close around her again, let it shield her and cool her. She began a lazy breaststroke, keeping her head above the water so she could get her bearings and enjoy the view.

She had only gone a few strokes when Gabe drew level and began to swim beside her. "There's a chef here at the lodge." He spoke briskly, the detached Gabe she felt safe with.

She breathed a sigh of relief at his change of subject.

"He's overseeing the installation of the kitchen and providing meals for the tradesmen and the few staff who are here. You can eat in the dining room with everyone else or get him to prepare something to take back to your chalet."

"A chef? That must thrill him, feeding a bunch of hungry manual laborers. Macaroni and cheese all round."

"Adam's a friend of mine. He wanted to do this. He gets a break on the resort, some time away from a few…issues that he's having. And the guys appreciate it, too. Just because someone swings a hammer doesn't mean they don't like good food."

"No. I know." Chastity swam a little faster. How about that? She'd just been told off by Gabe for being judgmental. The very worst part about it was that he was right. All the same, she could allow herself to resent him for it. Because if she was busy resenting him, she could put out of her mind those feelings, urgings, she'd had on the pontoon.

They walked from the water. As Gabe picked up his clothes, she veered across the sun-warmed sand toward her chalet.

"Can you do me one favor?" he asked, catching up to her, heedless of his bare chest, of the way his damp boxers clung to his hips.

She kept her eyes fixed straight ahead. "Depends on what it is."

"Tell me before you go swimming?"

She wanted to say no, but the earnestness in his voice stopped the word. Instead, she lifted a shoulder. "Okay."

"Promise?"

"Yes," she agreed on a reluctant sigh.

* * *

"Books?"

Gabe watched Chastity as she looked up, startled, from the page she was reading and seemed to take a moment to focus. Though she was sitting beside a large window, the early evening light was fading and she probably should have turned a lamp on.

He leaned a shoulder against her door frame. Her door had been open, so naturally he'd looked in. And seen her, legs curled beneath her in the armchair, engrossed in a book. "That's what was in your suitcase?" he said when she didn't respond.

She glanced at the nightstand beside her bed and the half dozen books haphazardly stacked on it. "Among other things."

She shrugged—a simple lift of a pale, bare shoulder beneath the white strap of her sundress. Nothing that should captivate him. But something had changed from the moment he'd seen her kneeling in her garden. Despite his best intentions he saw her differently, as something more than just a gold-digging Ice Maiden. He'd had to admit that even gold diggers had feelings and that Chastity just might be a woman with hidden strengths and vulnerabilities. That didn't mean he wasn't still going to get what he wanted, needed—a father's rights. Because he was determined that he be a part of his daughter's life and that she be a part of his. He wasn't going to lose any more of his family to this woman. But there were ways and means of achieving his ends; they didn't all have to be unpleasant or confrontational.

"I don't like to be caught without a book." Defiance and apology mixed in her voice.

"We're only here for a week."

"You think I should have brought more? In case it rains?" Her voice was deadpan and he couldn't figure out whether she was serious or teasing. Her full lips didn't so much as twitch, but an intriguing light danced in her eyes.

He watched her as he strolled into the room, noting how quickly that light disappeared as she uncurled her legs and placed her bare feet on the floor. The flight response? He needed to cure her of that.

She flicked out the skirt of her sundress, smoothing it over her thighs. He touched the top book in the stack and looked to her for permission. Another lift of that shoulder. Not captivating, he told himself firmly. Again. But he could see a slight, inviting hollow above her collarbone.

He picked up the first book, a thriller that had been recommended to him. He'd been meaning to read it, but never had time these days. Beneath it lay a couple of romances, beneath those a book of essays by a political columnist. And last the pregnancy journal he'd given her.

"Eclectic." And far more stimulating than the financial reports that constituted the bulk of his reading these days.

"I don't always know what I'll feel like," she explained.

"Well, do you feel like dinner?"

She glanced at her bare wrist, which showed a faint strip of paler skin, then scanned the walls of the chalet, looking for a clock, as if the time made a difference whether she was hungry or not.

"There are no clocks here," he supplied.

"And I'm guessing it's not just because the decorating isn't finished?"

"You're right. Because the point of the lodge will be for people to forget about time while they're here."

She stood. "It's working then. And yes, I do feel like dinner."

While she slipped her feet, with their berry-red toenails, into her sandals, Gabe crossed back to the door to wait for her. She ducked her head as she passed him. What was it going to take for her to relax in his presence? In the gentle warmth of the evening, they walked side by side along the forest edge. The sun hung low in the sky, burnishing the clouds with orange.

His cell rang. "Marco?" He spoke to his right-hand man as he walked beside Chastity, his attention only partially on the call. He finally pocketed the phone just as a plump wood pigeon flew past with its characteristic slow wing beats, heading into the trees. He and Chastity stopped in unison.

"Did you see where it went?" she asked.

"There." He pointed over her shoulder. "In the puriri tree. It's going for the berries."

She narrowed her eyes but kept scanning.

Gabe moved to stand behind her so he could put his arm over her shoulder and give her a line of sight. And though he was careful not to touch her, he sensed her tense up. "Out on the second branch from the bottom."

She wasn't the only one who'd tensed with their proximity. He'd caught the scent of her freshly shampooed hair and had a sudden urge to lower his face to the top of her blond head.

"I see it," she gasped. "Oh, look, there's another one."

He was the one who was supposed to be charming her, not vice versa. How much of this was an act? The Chastity who'd lived with his brother had been a glamorous socialite. Photos of her and Tom used to appear regularly in the social pages of magazines and newspapers. They'd epitomized city sophistication, had vacationed in the Greek Islands, attended gallery openings in Paris and operas in Rome. And yet here she stood beside him, delighting in the sight of a native bird feeding.

She glanced over her shoulder, caught him staring at her and her excitement leached away, to be replaced by a small frown. She started walking again, and Gabe matched his stride to hers.

"Both adults brood the egg. The female during the night and morning, then the male takes over for the afternoon and through the evening."

"You're not exactly subtle, are you?" She looked over her shoulder at him.

"Meaning?"

"Oh, please. Don't play innocent. The whole two-parents-sharing deal. Not to mention the 'Gee, with my font of knowledge won't I be a great Dad' angle."

"Can't be ignored."

"Yes, it can be." She looked away.

If she thought it was going to be that easy, she was sadly mistaken. He touched a deliberate hand to the small of her back as they entered the dining room. Nothing intrusive, perhaps a little possessive. Another not-so-subtle message. He was not about to let her shut him out. He needed her to get used to him, used to the sizzle that existed between them, because regardless of what she wanted, her future now included him. And he needed her to not feel threatened by him so that she'd stop looking for ulterior motives in everything he said and did. Even if they were there. And for a moment, when she neither stepped away nor tensed, he thought he was making progress.

But then he saw the apprehension in her face as she looked at the six men already seated at one of the dining tables. Apparently, he was only the lesser of two evils. He could live with that, and use whatever advantage it gave him.

He shifted his hand, laid it on her shoulder then, the one nearest to him so that his arm wasn't even around her back. He meant only to give it a reassuring squeeze, but he hadn't expected the silken feel of her skin to heat his palm.

She wasn't the only one who had to get used to the sizzle. He dropped his hand and touched it once more to the small of her back. Here at least was the protective barrier of fabric. He urged her forward. "They're good guys," he said quietly in her ear. She gave her head a quick shake that feathered her hair over her shoulders, and as she lifted her chin a transformation came over her. Uncertainty vanished and before his eyes, she became the Chastity of those social pages photos—bright, sophisticated, untouchable.

And yet he still wanted to touch her.

The men had looked up and were watching them. Her. He knew it was her, because men didn't generally forget to chew just because they were looking at him.

Dave, the foreman, lifted his chin by way of a greeting, then stood and pulled out the chair at the table next to him. Gabe was betting that also wasn't for his benefit. Chastity seemed to glide across the room. She stopped at their table.

"You guys are doing an amazing job on this place."

And six men started talking at once to try to tell her what they'd been doing. He watched in fascination and, he had to admit, admiration. The woman could work a room, or table, as it were.

After a few minutes he maneuvered her to the next table, before the men could shuffle up and make room for one more, monopolizing her.

Adam brought out their meals. Gabe was expecting the warm lamb salad that the others were eating. It took him a single horrified moment to recognize the meal the Paris-trained chef had set in front of Chastity was macaroni and cheese. He looked at Adam's impassive face. Although he'd shared Chastity's comment with him earlier, Gabe hadn't expected him to make anything of it. Adam was normally a customer service genius, allowing nothing and no one to get under his skin.

A small frown pleated Chastity's brow and then she laughed. Full on, stomach-holding laughter. She looked up at Adam who was now grinning from ear to ear.

The last thing Gabe expected was for Chastity to push her seat back so she could stand and embrace his chef. Nor for his chef to enfold her in a bear hug in return—a hug that in Gabe's opinion lasted far too long. It was his turn to frown.

Finally, Chastity stepped back, smiling widely and slowly shaking her head as she looked at Adam. "Wow. Look at you." She most definitely was, so Gabe did, too, trying to see what put that awed smile on her face. All he saw was Adam, part Maori, a little rough around the edges, his too-long dark hair tied back, a gold stud in one ear, a tattoo just visible beneath the sleeve of his T-shirt, encircling his biceps. He supposed some women would find him attractive in that living-on-the-edge kind of way. But he really wouldn't have thought Adam was the type Chastity would go for. He didn't smack of wealth, though that was deceptive. His restaurants had been phenomenal successes both in New Zealand and in London. Part of that success was due to the image Adam had created and perpetuated for himself as being a hell-raiser from the wrong side of the tracks.

"Wow, right back at you," Adam said tugging on a lock of Chastity's hair. "If Gabe hadn't told me your name, I don't think I would have recognized you for the skinny kid with hair almost green from too much chlorine. Of course the macaroni and cheese comment helped."

"Grab a chair, Adam," Gabe said. "You two clearly have some catching up to do." He pushed aside the relief that had swept through him at the realization that they knew each other from a long time ago. And, more importantly, hadn't seen each other since. Now might just be a good time to learn more about Chastity.

"Sorry, can't." Adam jerked his head in the direction of the kitchen. "Got stuff to do." He reached for Chastity's plate. "I'll bring out your proper dinner."

Chastity grabbed hold of her plate with two hands. "What, and miss out on the dish that started it all? No way."

Adam smiled and tugged her hair one more time. "Catch up with you tomorrow?"

"Of course."

Chastity watched Adam leave, and Gabe watched Chastity, studying the sweet reminiscent expression on her face. She turned slowly back to him and the expression vanished. With a small shake of her head she became Social Pages Chastity once more.

He wanted to know the other.

She ate a forkful of her pasta, heedless of the calorie-laden carbs, and the smile returned. She looked up and caught him watching her. "Adam grew up in the same place I did."

"I said my mother had another side. She's got nothing on you."

Chastity ignored the comment. "He had a hard time of it. People always expected the worst of him and his family." There was a subtle challenge in both her words and her eyes. She broke the gaze, blinking, and then looked over Gabe's shoulder at the bay behind him. She gave a small, sad laugh. "Often as not, he delivered. He's a couple of years younger than me, but he always made out that he was older and tougher. I found him one time down at the beach. Not so tough. He'd been beaten up. I was…going through a rough patch, too. We got to talking about how we were going to get away from that…town. Make something of our lives."

"Looks like you both did."

"I guess." She returned her attention to her food, eating with a deliberate and concentrated precision.

"Good macaroni?"

She smiled. "The best."

They talked a little more throughout the meal. Gabe kept the topics neutral, wanting her to relax. She was easy to talk with, but there was a measured quality to her conversation as though she weighed her words before she spoke, careful not to reveal anything she didn't want to. But each time she smiled or laughed at something he said, it felt like a victory to be savored.

Once they'd finished they chatted a while with the

workmen who were leaning back nursing beers, and then they left. Outside, they walked in unspoken agreement to the water's edge. A full moon hung in the sky, bright enough to cast shadows and shimmering on the still bay.

"Look at it." Chastity sighed over its beauty, but Gabe was far more captivated by the way the light caught softly on her hair and pale shoulders. She slipped off her sandals, letting them dangle from one hand as she walked ankle deep in the water in the direction of her chalet. With her other hand, she pulled up the skirt of her dress.

Gabe kept to the sand, keeping pace with her. Watching her. Wanting to know her, needing to pin down who it was that he was dealing with. "Where was this town you and Adam grew up in?"

"Nowhere you would have heard of," she said, not looking at him.

"Try me."

"No point. It's on the east coast, but not on the way to anywhere. No one who hasn't actually lived there has ever heard of it. Small town, small minds. At least back then."

"It's changed?"

"I wouldn't know. I left when I was seventeen."

"You've never been back?"

"No."

"What about your family?"

"Nothing to tell."

"A town I wouldn't have heard of. A family you have nothing at all to say about. Could you be any more evasive?"

She stopped in the water and turned to face him,

hands planted on her hips. "Fine. One mother, dead for six years. Two half sisters. No genetic diseases or deformities you need to worry about. All our vices are of choice. And, like I said, I didn't know my father. He left when I was a few months old, so I can't vouch for him. Is that enough for you?"

Not nearly. "Are you close to your half sisters?"

"If by close you mean have I spoken to them since our mother's funeral, then the answer's no."

"So you have no one?"

"I can take care of myself."

"That's not what I meant." What was she hiding behind that bristling defiance?

Her expression clouded. "I had my grandmother until a little under a year ago. She was an amazing woman." And then, as though regretting letting him see she'd cared about someone, as though it was a weakness, she lifted her chin and glared at him, and that sorrow he'd glimpsed in her eyes vanished. "Is there anything else you'd like to know?"

"Yes. How heavy is that chip you're carrying around on your shoulder?"

She paused. "Mostly I forget about the chip. Except when some privileged rich guy starts looking down his nose and asking questions, ready to judge me because of where I come from."

"By that, you mean me?" Gabe didn't react because he sensed old hurts beneath the insinuation.

"If the shoe fits."

"I don't judge a person on their upbringing or their past," he said quietly. "I'd like to think I don't judge at all."

Her silence was telling.

She turned away and started walking quickly through the foam of the lapping surf.

"Wait up." He wasn't surprised when she didn't. He kicked off his shoes, jogged along the beach then rolled up the legs of his pants and waded into the water, catching hold of her hand. "What did I say or not say that made you think I was judging you?"

She didn't look at him, just kept walking. Her hand lay utterly passive in his. "Nothing. It's just what people do. Particularly successful people from wealthy backgrounds. I moved away from there because I didn't want to be defined by my family." She made to pull her hand away and he tightened his grasp.

"No one wants to be defined by their family. I knew Adam's background had been tough. He's told me snippets, and I've met some of his family. I never thought it defined him."

"Maybe not. But a lot of people do and some definitions definitely look a lot better than others."

Was she aware that her fingers had curled around his?

"So, you think a judgmental snob from a wealthy background, as you're happily labeling me, is better than a woman who grew up poor but made something of herself?" He wondered what she'd had to overcome to become the woman she was today.

"You really have no idea." She faced him, standing close. "And you do make judgments. Everyone does."

There was nothing passive about her now. Energy leaped from her. And God help him he wanted to kiss her, to cover her mouth with his, to drink in the taste of her, fill his hands with her. To pull her hard against him. Why her? Why did this woman have this effect on him?

It was sorcery; he was under some kind of spell. He broke free of it, furious at his weakness. Furious at her. At himself. He opened his fingers, let go of her hand. Perhaps without the contact of skin, he'd get his head back on straight.

"Maybe. But if I were to judge someone it would be based on solid evidence—my own interactions with them and on their actions. On facts. Like marrying a man for his money, like coming between him and his family." The words were finally out in the open. He waited for her denial, watched carefully for her reaction.

The moon was full and bright, but not *that* bright and he couldn't read her expression. She drew herself up taller. "I'm not having this conversation. It can't achieve anything."

Gabe stared. That was it? Disappointment washed through him. If she'd said she married Tom for love he wouldn't have believed her, but he'd wanted her to at least have convinced herself that she did. He wanted the pretense rather than the mercenary silence of admission.

They walked toward her chalet, not together, but as two strangers who happened to be following the same path.

At the door to her chalet she paused and looked in his direction, not quite meeting his gaze. "Good night." Cool, haughty. Unrepentant. She slipped inside, vanishing from the night.

Seven

Chastity heard Gabe's voice before she saw him. So much for slipping into the back of the kitchen for lunch and a visit with Adam. She looked up in the direction of the surprisingly close sound and did a double take. If it had been up to her eyes alone, she probably wouldn't have seen him at all, or at least not recognized that it was him. He and Dave stood high above the ground on a scaffolding plank inspecting something on the roof.

She turned away from the sight of Gabe in worn, fitted jeans with a leather tool belt slung low across his hips, and kept walking. She'd planned on avoiding him today, had spent the morning reading and if she could leave her book alone this afternoon, would go for a walk or even try fishing. The weather wasn't as nice as it had been yesterday so she convinced herself she didn't have to swim—because swimming meant time, or at least communication, with Gabe.

Last night, needing to quash the strange stirrings of feeling she had for him, she had taken his accusations about her marriage without argument, but she wasn't ready or strong enough for more.

"Yo, Chastity!" Dave called out. "Lunchtime already? Wait up, we'll come with you."

Great. Looked like she didn't have a choice about being ready or strong enough. She watched the two men climb down from the scaffold.

Gabe would never have believed the truth, that she had married Tom because she had lost the last family member she felt any real connection to, that she was alone and lonely, because she didn't honestly believe in love—for her—not the soul-deep, lifelong connection touted in the movies. Tom had been kind and friendly and up-front about his reason for wanting marriage. Another reason Gabe would never believe.

Gabe jumped lightly to the ground.

"You two go ahead. I'll go round up the guys." With a smile in her direction, Dave disappeared.

Right. Good. Gabe drew level with her and they started walking. Forget about last night. Forget about the animosity. Forget about the strange other heat that had preceded it. Today was a new day, could hopefully be a neutral day. "When you said you'd be working, I didn't think you meant *working,* working."

He looked at her, relaxed and seemingly blessedly neutral. "As in manual labor?"

"Precisely."

"Judging me, Chass?" Okay, so he wasn't going to

forget about last night. But he said it with a half grin that softened his face. And so maybe at least he, like her, was moving forward, putting the past, both recent and more distant, behind him.

"Apparently."

"Actually," he continued, the grin stretching into a smile that spoke to something deep within her, "I didn't think I'd be doing this kind of work, either. But the lawyer who was coming out for a meeting had to reschedule for the afternoon and Dave was down a man this morning, so…" He shrugged, broad shoulders lifting casually beneath the soft cotton of a white T-shirt.

"You know what you're doing? With a hammer?"

"I know enough. I used to volunteer with a charity at building sites during summer vacations."

And suddenly it wasn't hard to imagine at all. Gabe was the sort who could do whatever he decided he'd turn his hand to. Another difference between the brothers. "Tom didn't."

"It wasn't Tom's thing."

She laughed at the thought. "It wouldn't have been. If there was anything that needed doing at the apartment, his first, his only, reaction was to call a tradesman. Several times I stopped him because it was something I could do myself."

"You?"

"Who's judging now?"

"We really do need to start again, don't we?"

"Maybe we just need to be a little more open-minded," she said.

"Maybe." They walked on a few steps. "I guess working on the building sites was my way of spending less time around home."

Was that an admission that the family life Tom found so stifling and repressive had also impacted Gabe? "From what I learned, Tom's way was partying." She could just imagine fun-loving Tom breezing through his summer vacations in a whirl of socializing.

"Something like that." The shadow of his grin still lurked as he opened the door to the restaurant and waited for her to enter.

She smiled up at him, remembering. "He was so easy to love." She regretted her words as the grin disappeared and his eyes narrowed on her. Her step faltered. Not like Gabe, who wouldn't be at all easy to know or to love. But wasn't there some saying about the things worth having not being easily attained?

He stood waiting, arm outstretched, still watching her. She sucked in a deep, supposedly fortifying, breath as she passed close to his masculine warmth, to the contours of his chest.

They ate in silence, her words apparently having killed the conversation. She put down her fork. "What if it wasn't me?"

"What if what wasn't you?"

"What if it wasn't me who drove a wedge in your family? You practically just admitted that you used work to avoid your family, too."

Gabe stared at her, intent. "You're saying it wasn't?"

She should never have spoken, but she had and so now had to continue. "I'm saying laying all the blame at my door is a cop-out." Tom had worked at avoiding his family. Yes, he'd used her as an excuse, at first without her knowledge, but even once she realized what he was doing she hadn't especially minded. And from what she saw, the family wasn't overly concerned. At least they hadn't been until Tom went and died on them all.

"You were all adults, capable of making your own decisions. It's just easier to blame someone else. You can't blame Tom because he's dead, you don't want to blame yourselves because that would mean accepting guilt, so you blame me."

"What were we supposed to assume when Tom said the two of you couldn't come to a family dinner because you'd made other arrangements, or you weren't feeling well, over and over till it was undeniably obvious that it was nothing more than a phony excuse?"

"How hard did you really try? So often the invitations were for Tom alone that it could be interpreted as nothing more than insulting. Do you blame him for sticking up for his wife? What effort did you personally make to see Tom outside of work, to try to understand where he was at?"

"What needed to be understood? He had a great job, a great life. And he had you."

Silence fell as he challenged her with his gaze. There was so much about Tom that Gabe had needed to understand. And now it was too late. But mainly she fixated on his last sentence. "And he had you." As though Tom's having her was…something Gabe envied?

The builders turned up then, arguing and joking, and soon Adam joined them, insisting that he have the seat next to Chastity. She felt finally like she had a friend at her shoulder, someone to shield her from Gabe. She turned to Adam, let him regale her with stories of his times in London and around the world.

When the helicopter touched down outside, Gabe excused himself from the table.

As conversation flowed around her, Chastity watched through the massive windows as he greeted the suited lawyer who stepped from the chopper, and she tried to figure out how it was that Gabe, in jeans and a T-shirt, was subtly, yet clearly, the man with the power.

She also tried to figure out why Gabe held an undeniable fascination for her, how he affected her on so many levels. She couldn't help but wonder, if things had been different… He'd invaded her thoughts, claimed her senses. She wanted to look at him, to touch him. She'd even, as she'd passed by him earlier, had the craziest urge to press her face to his chest and breathe in his scent.

But things weren't different, and the crazy compulsions were just, she told herself, repercussions from the knowledge that she carried his child. Maybe she was a vehicle for the unseen and unseeing person getting to know her father. Just as her appetite for food was a way to nourish the child, her appetite for Gabe was also stirred by the child.

Appetite for Gabe? She wanted to bang her head on the table.

"You look like you've got it bad."

Startled, Chastity turned to Adam. She'd forgotten he was even there. "I've got something bad, that's for sure. I just don't know what it is, or what I should do about it."

"I know the feeling."

"Woman trouble?" she smiled.

He nodded. "Man trouble?" he asked in return.

"Always is," they said in unison.

"This time," Adam said, "it's not something I can run away from."

Chastity looked back out at Gabe. He and the lawyer were striding across the lawn. He glanced in her direction, his gaze a direct contact despite the distance and the glass between them. This man was the father of her child. There was no running away from that fact. "Me neither."

Gabe watched Chastity across the table. The setting sun behind her burnished her hair as she finished her salmon and salad, and aligned her knife and fork neatly together on her plate. He hadn't seen her all afternoon. She'd reluctantly joined him for dinner, but had scarcely spoken to him, let alone looked at him. And yet when she talked to Dave or Adam, he caught glimpses of someone else, someone relaxed with a ready laugh and a dazzling smile.

She wore a white tank top with jewel-like stones studded around the neckline. A neckline that dipped low but clung faithfully. He knew because it had nagged at his attention all through their meal.

Chastity glanced around the dining room, her gaze sliding past him. "I think I'll head back to my chalet."

"Adam's made dessert."

"I'll pass." She stood, so Gabe did, too.

Surprise—or was it that latent fear he'd seen before?—crossed her face. Either way he made her edgy. "You stay."

He shook his head. "I'll walk with you."

He saw a protest form on her lips, but then she looked at him and whatever she'd been about to say died away.

She went for a nonchalant shrug instead, lifted her chin. A nonverbal *whatever.*

His phone rang and while he took the call, she made her escape.

But it was a quick call and he followed her outside. In the balmy evening she hesitated at choosing between the direct path to her chalet and the walk along the foreshore. She headed for the water. Sandals dangling from her fingers, she walked along the wet sand, heedless of the waves that periodically swept up and around her ankles.

He caught up easily, but she didn't acknowledge his presence. "I've been thinking about what you said at lunch, about the blame for Tom's estrangement not being yours."

"I've been thinking about it, too, and I'm sorry. I shouldn't have said what I did. I'm also sorry that you missed out on so much of Tom's life in the last two years."

"Who *are* you?" He unintentionally voiced his thoughts. She was such a puzzle, sometimes confirming his opinion of her, sometimes confounding it.

She paused and looked at him.

The more time he spent with her the less he felt he knew her. Two steps forward and two steps back, or sideways, ending up somewhere different but no more enlightening. Was it possible to confuse reserved and perhaps uncertain with haughty and cold? Just a few weeks ago he'd been so sure he knew her, or knew her type. An ever-climbing socialite, all gloss and no substance. But he was starting to wonder whether that wasn't precisely what she wanted him to think. Whether her refusal to defend herself last night was just that and no more? Too many things about her didn't quite add up. How did her friendship with

Sophie, her love of reading and swimming and walking barefoot in the water fit with the socialite persona?

"Who am I? What do you mean?" She was immediately defensive and he didn't want her defensive.

"Nothing." He had to be more subtle. Watch and wait for her to reveal herself.

"I've got a question then. Who are *you?* Does work really consume as much of your life as it looks like it does, as Tom always said it did?"

He thought about that for a moment. "Yes." It was the only honest answer. "But that's my choice. I could just as easily choose to do other things, as well. But work is what gets me fired up—the making of deals, seeing projects come to fruition." Although lately, if he was honest, he hadn't found the same satisfaction that he used to. "When I'm a father, that will change."

Chastity made a dismissive noise, almost a snort. Then when she looked at him, her derision turned to horror. "You really think you want to play Daddy?"

"It won't be playing."

She turned and kept walking. "I just have a hard time picturing you in the role."

Gabe narrowed the distance between them so that they walked almost shoulder to shoulder. "I don't find it so hard. I've been thinking about it a lot lately."

"And?"

"And I've realized I do want children. I just hadn't thought about it before because I haven't met the right woman. But I can imagine building sand castles at this very beach, walking along the sand with a woman, a child between us, each holding a hand, swinging my little girl over the waves." He allowed himself to picture the scene.

She was silent a moment as they walked slowly on. "There are so many things wrong with that picture."

"Like what?"

"Like you're picturing some idyllic time, forgetting things like sleepless nights and childhood illnesses and dirty diapers."

"I'm a realist if nothing else. I know about those things. Doesn't mean that has to be what I choose to dwell on. It's not what you think about, is it? You think about cuddles and gurgling laughter and butterfly kisses."

"I guess," she admitted. "But what about the woman part? You're already picturing a woman on the scene helping you. There might not be one. You'll likely be doing it all alone."

"I'm more than happy to, and capable of, doing it alone. But chances are there'll be a woman. A wife. At some stage."

A small frown pleated her brow as her gaze found his across the foot of evening that separated them, but he couldn't read what was in her eyes. "Is there someone?" she asked as though considering the possibility for the first time. "Does she know? About this?" Chastity gestured to her stomach.

"There's no one at the moment. But there will be one day. It's on my list."

"It's on your *list*?" A gurgle of laughter, like sunlight on water, escaped her. "What, somewhere between 'buy next resort' and 'pick up dry cleaning'? Like when you get to number six on your list, you'll look around and the perfect woman will be waiting?"

"That didn't come out quite how I meant it."

"No, but it was probably how you were thinking it. And I've seen the women you date. They might not be so keen on Bachelor of the Year if he has a little girl taking up too much of his time and attention."

"That's not the kind of woman I'll marry."

"Just the kind you like to sleep with."

He ran his hand through his hair in frustration. "You are so twisting this."

"You're doing a pretty good job of that on your own."

"You know nothing about the women I've dated."

"Aside from all the cosmetic surgery," she cupped and lifted her breasts, momentarily riveting his attention there, "and Amber who never got her hair wet when she swam."

He dragged his gaze upward. "Amber who was a pediatric oncologist."

"Was she really?" Surprise sprang to her face and he felt momentarily bad for tricking her.

"No. Sadly, she was actually a lingerie model."

"Really?" And this time she sounded intrigued.

"No. Sorry again. I was joking."

She looked away.

He slung his arm around her stiff shoulders and leaned in. Brotherly, he tried to tell himself. He wasn't going to let her dismiss him on any level. "Are you always this gullible?"

"Pretty much. It's a failing." The shoulders softened beneath his touch. And for the life of him, he couldn't force himself to drop his arm. He barely managed to stop his fingers from caressing the warmth of her skin.

"It's a very endearing failing."

She looked back at him, a very endearing earnestness in her gaze. "Anyway, back at your apartment that first night, you said you never joked."

"I don't. Usually." What was it about being with her that changed him? And why? He thought again about dropping his arm, and just as quickly dismissed the thought. There was no harm in it. Friends.

"This woman on your list, what does she do, what does she look like?"

"She's a kindergarten teacher."

Chastity laughed, the sound dancing over the waves.

"Actually I wasn't joking that time."

She laughed harder, her slender frame shaking beneath his touch.

In one movement Gabe snaked a leg out in front of her ankles and pivoted her so that she fell backward till the only thing keeping her from the water were his arms, one behind her shoulders, one around her waist. Her hands flew to his shoulders, clutched at him.

"Not so funny now, is it?" He met her deep blue eyes, mere inches away from his, the laughter still dancing there. His gaze flicked to her softly parted lips. And he wanted nothing more in all the world than to haul her against him and kiss her. To lose himself in her. To lose both of them. Forget everything except this moment. Not brotherly. Not friendly. Something else altogether, something hot and insistent.

He righted her again, released her and walked slowly on as though nothing at all had happened. As though his world hadn't tripped and tilted in much the same way he'd done to her. He wanted Chastity Stevens. Wanted himself deep inside her.

And that wanting could only lead to disaster.

She caught up to him. "But a kindergarten teacher? Really?"

Gabe fought for composure. Ruthlessly quashed the erratic, erotic thoughts. "Doesn't have to be. That was just an example."

"Someone wholesome and innocent." A shadow passed over her face.

"No, someone kind and gentle and trustworthy."

The shadow deepened.

"Though I don't have a problem with wholesome and innocent."

"And why would Miss Kind-Gentle-Trustworthy-Wholesome-and-Innocent want to have anything to do with Mr. Ruthlessly-Successful-Workaholic? Aside from money? Which naturally she won't care about. When are you even going to find time to locate this perfect woman?"

"I'll make time."

"You're what, thirty-four? And you haven't made time yet."

"I've been busy. I haven't felt the need."

"You've been busy your whole life. It's not that easy to stop."

"I can stop whenever I want."

"The world will keep turning if you take a step back from it."

"A fact I'm well aware of, thank you." His phone rang, and he clenched his fists to stop himself from reaching for it.

"Then give me your phone."

"No." He let the call go to voice mail.

"Why not?"

"People need to be able to contact me. I need to be able to call them, arrange things."

Chastity's eyes danced with merriment and superiority as she…smirked.

"It's not that I can't."

She nodded, ostensibly agreeing. "When did you last take a vacation?"

"That's none of your business."

An I-told-you-so look of satisfaction spread across her face. "When were you last separated from your phone for more than an hour?"

"This conversation is ridiculous. You think you know me. You have no idea."

"Ditto," she said quietly. Then a little louder, "Here you are building this exclusive lodge so people can take some real time out, no clocks, no newspapers, the beautiful ocean at their doorstep, the simple pleasures of life and you can't even do it yourself."

"It's not a good time at the moment." He was well aware of both the irony and the flimsiness of his excuse. Chastity's eye roll proved she was aware of it, too.

"Children don't wait till it's convenient to need you. Prove that you can do it. Give me your phone."

His hand tightened around it in his pocket.

"Spend an entire day without it. Show me that you can."

He wasn't sure how she was somehow making this about him, as though he was the one who needed to prove himself worthy to be a parent. He didn't have to prove anything to her. Except that he deserved rights when it came to his child. But it could work both ways.

He pulled the phone from his pocket, and after checking who the last call had been from, switched it off and held it out to her. The surprise in her eyes was some consolation. She really hadn't thought he'd do it. Slowly, she reached out and took his phone, held it carefully yet gingerly.

Gabe slid his hands into his pockets. "If I'm going without my phone or work for the day, what do you have to do?"

"Keep you honest."

"Not good enough. You can go without your disguise."

"Disguise?" she sounded genuinely confused.

"The glamour, whatever. The makeup, the hairstyle, the designer clothes." Her eyes widened, making her look both startled and vulnerable. "It's all about simplicity, right?" She took a step away from him and he saw the *no* form on her soft pink lips. "Don't tell me you can't," he challenged, suddenly wanting this, and not just because it would even the balance of the challenge, but because there was someone different beneath the glamour, someone she only let him get glimpses of. But the glimpses intrigued him and he was curious, more than curious, to explore them.

"Of course I can, but—"

"Good. It's a deal." He knew better than to give her time to dwell on it or back out. "So, how are we spending this day?" It was his turn to push. "You and me. Together." He held her gaze, expecting that subtle fear he sometimes caught, but instead her eyes reflected her acceptance of the challenge and he saw a switch from defensive to offensive. He tamped down the flare of admiration and anticipation.

"You start by sleeping in. Then when you wake up you have coffee and breakfast brought to your chalet."

"No staff for that." He took pleasure in pointing out the first flaw in her plan.

"I'll do it." She smiled sweetly, countering him. "Then you sit in your pajamas—"

"I don't wear them."

"Or a bathrobe, or a pair of boxers," she said, after only the briefest hesitation. "Anything that's not proper clothes. You wear that while you sit on the veranda of the chalet eating your breakfast slowly and drinking—sipping—your coffee. Doing nothing other than enjoying the food, each and every bite you put in your mouth," she said, apparently unaware of the sensual images she conjured. "And appreciating the sight of the blue ocean in front of you, and the sound of the birdsong behind you."

"And you'll be with me?"

"Absolutely. Someone has to make sure you don't cheat, don't borrow a phone or a laptop. And obviously I'll have to have your laptop, too."

"Obviously," he said, not meaning it. "Then what?"

"Then nothing."

"What do you mean nothing?"

"I wouldn't have thought there were too many interpretations."

"But—"

"Oh, we'll do something. Probably. But the point is not to have it all planned out, not to schedule your time. We're not watching a clock." She gave a lazy shrug of her pale shoulder. "We might swim or read a book or go for a walk. Or we might do nothing. No thing. And you don't need to look so horrified. If you're going to have days where you have *my* child, then there will most definitely be days when you get absolutely nothing done—when if you manage to have a shave in the morning, you'll count that as an achievement."

"I hardly think so."

"Ever spent time around a baby?"

"No."

"Then let's just start with tomorrow, okay?"

"Sure."

She spun around, her skirt spinning and lifting with the movement, showing long, slender legs. "I'll see you with breakfast, then."

"What time?"

She laughed. "This is so going to kill you."

Eight

Chastity was far from laughing the next morning when she set the breakfast tray down on the outdoor table and tapped on the door of Gabe's chalet. Suddenly her brilliant idea seemed positively dimwitted. She'd backed herself into spending the day with Gabe. A Gabe who wouldn't have work to distract him. And somehow he'd known that without her careful facade of elegance she would feel vulnerable.

"It's open."

Like she'd step willingly into the lion's den? "I'll wait out here." She thought she heard his quiet chuckle. He was going to make her pay. A few seconds later his door swung open. The sunlight streaming onto the veranda caught on his bare chest, on the definition of his abs. Black silk boxers rode low on his lean hips. She dragged her gaze upward to his tousled hair, his beard-shadowed jaw, to his slumberous eyes. Chastity swallowed past the sudden dryness of her throat. "Have you really been in bed till now? Or is this a careful ruse and you've actually been up for hours secretly working?"

He stepped back so that she could see the unmade bed. "It's still warm if you want to test it."

"No. Thank you."

His gaze returned her assessment, traveled over her freshly scrubbed face, over the loose tank top, over her shorts, bare legs and the flip-flops on her feet. "Like the outfit."

"Thank you," she said, studying the wooden decking beneath her feet.

He tapped a gentle knuckle to the underside of her jaw urging her to look at him. "So what's for breakfast? I'm starving."

For a moment their eyes locked and her body heated. Chastity forced her legs to move and stepped back so that he could see the tray on the table. Gabe strolled past her.

She carried his child. The thought ricocheted around inside her. And there was a part of her—the part that could ignore the untold complications that fact caused—that was glad of it. It was only, she told herself, that on a purely primal level he was...her ideal of physical perfection.

Gabe sat, leaning back in his chair. "Everything okay?"

She shook her head to clear it. "Fine."

A knowing smile tugged at the corners of his lips. "Coffee?" He lifted the French press from the tray.

"No, thanks. There's a chamomile tea there for me." Though she was well beyond the point where the supposedly relaxing chamomile could give her any help.

"So, are you joining me?" He looked at her where she still stood by his door, one hand gripping the frame. She released her fingers, gritted her teeth and made her way to the second chair. Gabe passed the plate of melon slices to her. "Is something wrong?"

She could hardly tell him to put a shirt on without breaking her own rules of the day being about informality or worse, without revealing quite how distracting that bare chest, with its light covering of hair, was. "No." She picked up a slice of honeydew melon and bit into it.

When she looked up again he was staring at her. "What is it?"

"You have beautiful skin," he said with a note of surprise.

"Thank you. I think."

"You don't need all the makeup you wear. You don't need anything."

"My choice."

"What is it you're hiding?"

"Don't try to make it into something it's not." What she really meant was, *don't delve, don't try to figure out anything about me.* She wanted to keep her barriers against him, wanted even now to run back to her chalet, fix her face and her hair, change her clothes, because there was safety in the facade she presented to the world.

He shrugged. "I like it."

They lay on sun loungers in the shade of the veranda. Gabe was seemingly immersed in his—her book, the thriller, the one she'd planned on starting today. But when she'd brought out a selection for him to choose from, he'd gone straight for that one. She'd heard it was good. Sadly, the one she'd chosen for herself just wasn't grabbing her. For that the blame lay in part with the man a few feet away. The man turning the pages with great rapidity, the man who chuckled occasionally. The man with those long legs that were more enticing than the words on the page in front of her. Fortunately, he'd put on cargo shorts and a dark polo shirt after breakfast. The shirt at least saved her from his chest though it still managed to hint at the contours it shielded.

She tried her book for a couple more minutes before looking over at him again. "Shall we go snorkeling?"

It was a few seconds before he looked up. His gaze came to rest on her. "Sorry? Did you say something?"

"I thought you might like to go snorkeling. Adam says the next bay around is great for it. And I want to collect some shells for Sophie—those ring-shaped ones that fit over her fingers."

"No, I'm…" He checked out the book open in her hands, where she was clearly only a scant way into it, "Sure. Sounds good."

This wasn't how it was supposed to be working. He was the one who was supposed to be getting antsy at the enforced relaxation, not her. Still, she jumped up, discarding her book on her lounger. Gabe closed his book, set it on the floor and stood. He lifted his arms above his head, stretching. That chest was too close. Too inviting.

Gabe watched Chastity rest her dessert spoon on the side of her plate. He loved watching her eat, the sensory pleasure she took in food. He'd noticed it these past days. No picking at her meals, just her own brand of careful savoring. Often on her first mouthful she would even close her eyes, devoting all her attention to the flavors in her mouth.

She looked up, caught him watching her. "So, how'd you find it? A whole day without your cell phone?"

"Remarkably pleasant." And it had been, if he ignored the constant thrum of physical awareness. Reading, snorkeling, swimming, even a siesta. He couldn't remember the last time he'd spent such an indolent day. He couldn't remember the last time he'd spent such an easy day with a woman. It had been Chastity who needed time to relax into it, but finally she had when they'd gone fishing. Her wariness around him had receded and they'd talked, or not, as they sat on the end of the jetty, helped each other with the fish they finally caught. He liked that she wasn't squeamish. He liked that his fish had been bigger than hers and that that had subtly annoyed her. Funny how he could like having her both relaxed and unaware of him and like getting under her skin.

In the fading light they walked along the beach. Chastity *in* the water as usual. Gabe fingered the shell rings in his pocket.

When they were even with her chalet, she stopped and kicked up a small splash of water with her toes. "It's still so warm."

He heard the wistfulness in her voice. "You want to swim again, don't you?"

"Yes." She looked at him. "Do you mind? I know you don't want me swimming without you watching. But it'll be safe. There's light left and the moon is already up. I love swimming at night. It's so...otherworldly."

Just as she was, standing there like a mythical goddess in human form with the water lapping around her calves. A siren sent to tempt and bewitch him.

"Swim. I don't have anywhere else I have to be. Unless you're letting me off the hook now and giving me back my phone?"

"Nope. One whole day. That was the deal. I'll just change." She skipped from the water and jogged toward her chalet. Gabe breathed a sigh of pure relief.

He was waiting for her when—bikini clad—she came back out. He caught her scanning the shoreline and looking back toward the chalets. "Gabe?" she called. Her soft voice carried across the water.

"Here."

She spun to face the bay where he trod water, waiting for her.

"Oh."

"I wanted to be close. So I didn't lose sight of you."

"I didn't mean to make you swim, too."

"It's no hardship." The hardship lay in watching her standing there hesitant in the moonlight, her pale limbs long and slender. She walked slowly into the water. He swallowed and turned away. Good thing the water and darkness hid his reaction to her. If she was anyone else, if he didn't know the things he did about her, if they didn't both have agendas, if she hadn't been his brother's wife... He swam a few lazy strokes deeper. *Stay in control here,* he warned himself.

He heard the quiet splash of her stroke as she caught up to him. They breaststroked in unison toward the jetty and stopped a few meters shy of it and trod water. Over the lap of the waves on the shore, they heard the occasional burst of laughter from the men still in the dining room. Gabe looked toward the sound—away from her pale face and shoulders, away from the swell of her breasts just visible beneath the waterline.

The dining room was the brightest spot of light on the shoreline, and he could make out the men sitting inside. Through a second window he could see Adam with a phone pressed to his ear. Adam—who knew Chastity. The more time Gabe spent with her, the less he felt like he knew her. He looked back at her. And wanted her.

"Why Tom?" That easily he shattered their fragile truce.

She backed away a little, putting physical distance, as well as emotional distance, between them. "I thought you'd already decided the answer to that. For his money. Maybe what you really mean is why did he marry me?"

He said nothing.

"Oh, right. You've decided the answer to that, as well."

He wouldn't be swayed by the hurt in her expression and looked away, toward her chalet, just one solar-powered outdoor light indicating its location. When he turned back she was no longer beside him. He waited, then turned a frantic full circle, and when he still didn't locate her, panic flared. "Chastity?"

Nothing.

"Chass!" he shouted.

Still nothing. He was about to shout again before diving down to search when he heard the faintest splash. He spun toward the sound to see her surfacing halfway to the shore and swimming in her graceful freestyle for the beach.

Gabe surged after her.

She had a big enough head start that she'd reached water shallow enough to walk in by the time he caught up with her, and she was pushing through the waist-deep ocean.

He caught hold of her wrist. "Don't do that to me."

She turned, pulling her wrist from his grasp. "Do what?"

"Disappear in the water."

She looked up at him, her eyes sparkling with anger in the moonlight. "I'll do what I please. I'm not a child and I'm not your responsibility. And I'm not going to wait passively around while you insult me."

When she would have turned away he grabbed her shoulders. "You're here with me, you are my responsibility. And you're carrying my child."

"Don't pretend you care."

"I do care. You frightened me." He could barely keep the anger from his voice. He'd never known panic like those infinite few seconds when he couldn't see her.

Some of the fight went out of her, he could feel it in the softening of her shoulders beneath his hands. "I'm not going to do anything that could harm your child, because first and foremost she's my child."

"It's not just the baby."

"Oh, please. If it wasn't for the baby, you and I would never have seen each other again. You can't stand me. That much is obvious despite your halfhearted efforts at hiding it. I know what you're trying to do. But give it up because—"

He cut her words off with his kiss. Dammit. He couldn't help himself. Without thought he'd lowered his mouth to hers. Her lips were cool and salty from the water, but her mouth was hot and open beneath his because he'd caught her midsentence. And he couldn't stop. With his hands still on her shoulders, he pulled her closer till their bodies pressed together in the water. He tasted her sweetness, reveled in the soft contours of her body—breasts, hips, thighs—and he felt her response coursing through her. Her body communicating directly with his. Her hands clasped his head, her fingers threaded through his hair and her tongue moved against his. He was in heaven, a deep, drugging ecstasy that obliterated all thought, left only sensation and desire. He could feel the press of her breasts against his chest and he groaned his helplessness into her mouth, eased his thigh between her legs and she bore down against him.

Her hands shifted to his shoulders and for a second she clung fiercely to him, and then she flattened her palms and pushed. She stepped away, turned and surged through the water. Gabe watched her go. Watched her run for her chalet as soon as she hit the sand. Watched her open her door, heard her slam it behind her.

What had he done?

Kissing Chastity hadn't been part of his plan. He wasn't even supposed to like her. She'd trapped his brother. She was a mercenary, conniving, manipulative, beautiful...fragile, sweet woman who had let his family vilify her to protect Tom, and who was carrying his baby. And who kissed like she was on fire. For him.

And he wanted her.

His dead brother's wife. Gabe knew right from wrong and this was wrong on so many levels. He wanted to blame her. She shouldn't have kissed him back. But he couldn't. He'd started the kiss, caught her by surprise and she had ended it. He tried to tell himself that he wished she'd ended it sooner, but he was only grateful that she hadn't.

* * *

Chastity couldn't identify the sound that woke her at first. When she finally recognized it for a helicopter, she leaped from her bed. The helicopter meant escape. A way off this island without having to wait for the mail ferry—the option she'd settled on as she'd tossed, sleepless, through the night.

She raced to her window in time to see the chopper lift into the air—leaving, not arriving.

At breakfast she made the discovery that Gabe had gone with it. He'd left no message. He obviously wanted to get away from her. He must have felt her response last night. Her hunger for him.

Stupid. That's what she'd been. Seven kinds of stupid.

If and when he came back she'd be ready for the helicopter. She had to get away from here. Away from him.

Adam found her reading on a sun lounger after lunch. "There's a path that leads up through the forest. Takes about half an hour."

Chastity dropped her book, jumping at the chance to do something different. Something that might distract her. The book, the thriller she'd snagged back from Gabe, had scarcely held her attention. It had scant power in comparison to the memory of last night, of Gabe's kiss, and of the desire that had flamed through her.

She pulled her sundress on over her swimsuit. Adam would be good company. He would ask no questions.

Instead, she found, it was her who had questions. "How do you know Gabe?"

"We've been friends for years. Ever since I catered a function for him in London."

"What's he asked you about me?"

"Gabe?"

She nodded.

Adam looked blank. "Nothing."

"Nothing about where we grew up?" She didn't need to spell it out for Adam—about her childhood full of taunts, about the town that had shunned her because of whose daughter, and whose sister, she was. "My family?"

"No. And even if he had, I wouldn't have said anything."

"I know that. I just thought he'd try to probe."

"If Gabe had questions, he'd ask you. That's how he is."

She acknowledged his point. Gabe had no trouble asking direct questions.

They were standing at the lookout on the island's highest peak and admiring the 360 degree view when she first heard and then saw the returning chopper.

"Oh, no." She turned for the track.

"What?" Adam called after her, alarmed.

"I need to catch that helicopter." Her case was packed in preparation, ready and waiting at the door of her chalet. She ran—sprinted—back down the forested trail and burst into the open just as the helicopter disappeared out over the ocean again. She wanted to scream her frustration.

Standing in front of her was Gabe.

Adam came out of the forest and stood at her shoulder. "Everything all right?"

Gabe walked toward them. "Fine," she panted. "I've just got to go." She hurried toward her chalet. Hopefully he'd talk to Adam. Hopefully he wanted to avoid her as desperately as she needed to avoid him.

But she'd scarcely shut her door behind her when

Gabe knocked and pushed it open. He stood in the doorway, a white business shirt on, the top few buttons undone, lines etched into his face. Concern showed in his dark eyes.

"We need to talk." His gaze swept the bare room, paused at her case. "Planning on going somewhere?"

She, too, looked at the case. "Home. It's not working, me being here with you."

"You don't have to go."

"Yes, I do."

"I brought you here to rest, relax. And so we could get to know each other. I never meant... It was wrong. *I* was wrong. It won't happen again. I promise."

"You can't make that promise."

"I'm not that weak. I can and I will promise."

She looked at him then, held his gaze. "It wasn't just you, though, was it? There were two of us in that kiss."

His eyes narrowed warily. "I started it. I won't do it again." She could hear anger and blame, directed at himself, in his words.

She closed the distance between them. "I know you're not weak. But what if I am?" She caught his masculine scent. "What if I kissed you? Are you strong enough for both of us?"

"What?" His surprise was almost comical.

She turned away, walked to the vase of orange tiger lilies on the dresser. She touched a finger to the soft petals. "There's something you should know."

Gabe didn't say anything. As far as she could tell, he hadn't even moved. But he was listening. She knew it. "It's about Tom and me. About our relationship."

"I don't need to know anything about it. I didn't

before. I don't now." He couldn't disguise the tension and anger in his voice.

"Yes, you do. I need you to trust me because I'm going to be raising your—our—child. You already think badly enough of me. I'm not going to add this to the list. And you don't have to think as badly about yourself as I think you might be." She took a deep breath and looked at the flowers in front of her. "Tom and I, we didn't…we weren't…" she began, then took another even deeper breath. "We never slept together." The words rushed out.

She heard him move then. Quick footsteps. She turned in time to see him drop heavily onto her bed. "What? Why? No?" He looked at her in patent disbelief.

"Yes." She sat next to him, kept a careful distance and stared at her feet. "I'm not going to give you our reasons. They're private." Of all the things Tom had hidden from his family, that was the biggest. "But I just wanted you to know so you didn't think I was some kind of…"

"Never?" The question was laced with incredulous disbelief.

"Never," she said quietly. "And don't think that means I cheated on him. I didn't. I wouldn't."

"But what did you do for… Never mind."

"Sex?"

"It doesn't matter. Forget I asked."

"That's the easy part to answer. I never found sex to be all that it was cracked up to be. I'm quite happy without it."

His jaw dropped open and she smiled.

"I think it's maybe a lack of the normal hormones or something. Because usually I never even think about it.

The trouble is that's kind of changed since I've been pregnant. And lately I do think about it. A lot. And the real trouble is I think about it…with you. Even now, this very moment. You're sitting on my bed and I'm thinking about it, about you. So, you see, I need to leave."

"Damn."

"Exactly."

He stood, as though not wanting to be so close to her, as though worried, given her admission, that she'd try to jump him. Sensible man.

"Can you get the helicopter to return?" She spoke to his broad back as he stared out her window. Noted against her will his lean hips. His very nice, clutchable butt.

"Not till tomorrow. The pilot's on another job."

"The ferry?"

"Doesn't come Sundays."

"Oh."

He turned. "We can manage this."

"You'll have to do the managing because you're at least not being driven nuts by hormones."

"You at least have an excuse."

She didn't get his meaning. "Maybe if I slept with someone…other than you, the cravings would pass."

He said nothing. A muscle worked in his jaw.

"Adam might help me."

"Over my dead body."

"You're right. We spent too much time together growing up. He's too much like a brother."

"That's got nothing to do with it. If you're going to sleep with someone, it's going to be me."

In the echoing silence that followed his fierce pronouncement, she stared at him.

"You're having my baby anyway," he added.

"I'm not going to be your pity—"

"It wouldn't be pity, Chass. It'd be desire. The same thing you're fighting."

"Yes, but you're fighting it because you don't like who I am. I don't want to sleep with a man who doesn't like me. And I won't. I just won't. I'm not like—"

"Like who?"

"No one." She pushed past him. "I'm going for a swim. That will cool me off. And you are not swimming with me. And tomorrow I'm going to leave." She strode outside and across the sand. At the water's edge she peeled her dress off from over her swimsuit, dropped it on the sand and ran into the water. When she was chest deep, she turned to see that he'd followed her. "Don't come in. I'm not going any deeper than this." She swam for a hundred strokes parallel with the shore, turned and swam back again. All the while Gabe kept pace with her on the land.

When she stood again she was cold, deliciously cold, some of the awful, restless heat had gone. She walked from the water. "Actually, I think I'm better now. My little…problem has passed. But it will still be best if I leave tomorrow."

Chastity woke from a fevered dream in a tangle of sheets, the need within her almost unbearable. There was only one thing that seemed to help. Actually, there would be two things that would help, but she wasn't going near the second one.

Her one-piece swimsuit was still a little damp so she pulled on her bikini, threw a T-shirt over the top of it and in the half-light that preceded sunrise, she walked the short distance to Gabe's chalet. Promises. Why did she make them?

"Gabe," she whispered loudly. She tapped on his door. It swung open just as she was about to try the handle. He wore only boxers. The soft light of dawn washed over him, all contours and shadows. His gaze traveled over her, eyebrows rising as he took in her loose T-shirt, her bare legs. "I need to swim again," she whispered, embarrassed. She saw him swallow. "I'll be okay on my own though if you want to go back to bed."

"I'll change and come with you," he said, his voice raspy with sleep.

She turned, headed for the moonlit water. "I won't go in far this time, either. You don't need to come in," she called back over her shoulder.

"Don't look, but I could use a cold swim, too."

She looked and tried not to be awed and a little flattered. "Me?" she whispered.

Gabe was not amused. "Only you."

Really? Best not to dwell on that. These feelings—yearning, craving, hunger—were a temporary insanity. Chastity turned away again and dropped her T-shirt and her towel to the sand. She ran for the water and dived under as soon as it was deep enough. She swam. And when she finally stopped and looked for Gabe he was a distance—a safe distance—away. She swam for the pontoon, figuring that because Gabe was in the water, too, he wouldn't mind her being out so far. She touched it, then headed back for the shore, pushing herself hard. By the time she could touch her feet to the sandy bottom, she was tired and had cooled and most importantly had exorcised with exercise the fevered longing.

Gabe already stood on the shore, drying himself off. As she approached he picked up her towel and held it out to her. He was so beautiful.

"Better?" he asked.

"Yes. You?" She reached for the towel.

"Completely." He didn't let it go.

They stood facing each other, his gaze held hers. And the heat returned. She remembered the last time they'd been in the water together.

"I don't know what it is about your collarbone," he said.

"My collarbone?"

Gabe ran a finger along the bone, from her shoulder, over the strap of her bikini top, to the hollow at the base of her throat. The finger began its slow exploratory journey back and again encountered the strap. This time it slid beneath the thin strip of Lycra, eased it to the edge of her shoulder.

He gently thumbed where the strap had lain. Chastity stood, rendered immobile as he lowered his mouth to that very spot and pressed heated lips to her cold skin.

"Two choices. Water or bed?"

"Water," she croaked, grasping for the tattered shreds of her sanity, hoping it would douse the desire.

He eased her strap back into place then took her hand, led her back to the water. Chest deep, they stopped.

"Is this working for you?"

Mute, she shook her head.

"Me neither."

"Swimming might help?"

"It might."

He didn't release her hand though. Instead he turned toward her and tugged her closer till her breasts grazed against his chest, till her hips pressed against his and she could feel just how much it wasn't working for him. He slid his hands along her jaw, threaded his fingers into her hair. For a second he held her gaze and she could see the echo of her own hunger in his darkened eyes. And then he lowered his head.

Nine

Gabe's mouth was hot on hers, his kiss kindling the flames within her into an inferno. Chastity clutched at his shoulders and then, as his tongue danced with hers, slid her arms around him, needing to get closer. Needing to feel every part of him against every part of her. She wanted him. Desperately. He was strength and power and heat. He was solidity in a world that was spiraling. He was the only thing that made sense in the midst of her insanity.

For so long she had denied the way she wanted him, and then when she'd had no choice but to acknowledge her desire, she'd thought she would be strong enough to fight the clamoring need. Only now, she realized her utter weakness for him. All the willpower she had was focused not on running from him, but on getting closer, on sating her desire by claiming him in the most elemental of ways.

His seeking hands explored the length of her back, trailing sparks along her spine and over her skin. Those deft, pleasuring hands lowered till they cradled her hips, fingertips digging in to her buttocks, massaging, as he lifted and pulled her harder against him.

Buoyed by the water, Chastity lifted her legs, wrapped them around his hips and felt the delicious pressure of him against her. Closer. Better. And yet still not enough.

She tipped her head back as he trailed kisses down her throat, devoting himself for a time to her collarbone before his mouth moved hungrily lower. She hadn't realized he'd undone the strap of her bikini till the triangles of fabric covering her breasts fell away with the slightest tug of his teeth, revealing her tautly peaked nipples.

She should have felt vulnerable, and yet she felt like a goddess. He covered one nipple with his hot mouth, working dark magic with his lips and tongue and teeth, and she arched into him, a whimper escaping her. It was as though there was a direct line between her nipple and the swollen, aching flesh between her legs. And all the attention he lavished on her breasts only intensified her cravings. She pressed herself harder against him. She hadn't known need the like of it. Hadn't even known a need this powerful, this all-consuming, existed. She had to do something to ease it. And the only release to be had was with Gabe. Gabe, who should have been all wrong, but who was so very right.

She slid her hand between them, slid it inside the waistband of his swimming trunks, closed her fingers around the length of him and freed him. She nudged aside the narrow fabric of her bikini and positioned him at her entrance.

"Chass, wait." The raw weakness of his voice thrilled her. His grip was fierce on her hips.

"No. I won't. I can't. This is just sex. We both know that." She knew what she wanted. And what she wanted was Gabe. Only Gabe.

She touched a finger to his lips, silencing any further protests. He sucked the finger in, tugging hard on it, and she sighed with pure pleasure as, giving in to the demands of her body, she lowered herself onto him. She slid him in deep, stretching over the glorious length of him, till she was filled with him. *This* was what she needed. *He* was what she needed.

He pulled her on harder still. For a second they paused in wonder and pleasure, her gaze locked on his, and then at last he was moving, thrusting into her, guiding her hips to meet his. As she slid her arms around his shoulders, he again lowered his lips to cover her damp breast with his hot mouth as he rocked with her.

And she was so primed with need that that was all it took. Just that.

She cried out as her climax took her, surging outwards from her very center.

As the shock waves spilled convulsively through her, Gabe kissed her again, and she felt his release pulsing into her.

Afterward he wrapped his arms around her and held her to him in the water. She dropped her head to his shoulder, sated. And waited to come back fully into the world.

Slowly, sanity returned, and along with it came humiliation. What had she done? Who had she been for that brief, exquisite time? She eased off him. When he lifted his hands and retied her bikini top, she looked steadfastly over his shoulder, fixing her gaze on her chalet. The first rays of sun were touching the forest canopy. A light came on in a chalet at the other end of the bay where the workmen were staying. Wordlessly she started to move away. Gabe grabbed her hand, turned her back to him. And when she didn't look at him, he placed gentle fingertips beneath her chin and tilted her head up.

"I think we need to talk."

"I think we don't."

Ignoring her assertion, he kept hold of her hand, led her from the water toward her chalet. Inside, she moved to stand at the window overlooking the bay. He stood right behind her. Waiting. She could sense him. "I told you I should have left."

Silence settled over them. Neither of them moved.

"I'm sorry," she finally said.

His hand came to rest on her shoulder, warm, comforting—almost. And then he turned her, and again when she would have avoided his gaze, he tipped her head up so that short of closing her eyes, she had no choice but to look at him. "Don't be sorry. It wasn't your fault."

She allowed herself a small smile. "So, when I…took hold of you, slid onto you, while you were saying wait, that wasn't my fault?"

He smiled back. His hand cupped her jaw. "I started it. I kissed you. And I could have stopped you if I'd really wanted." His dark, unreadable eyes were intent on her. "But I didn't stop you because I didn't want to. Not even a little bit. So don't blame yourself."

"It was just sex. I remember saying that."

His hand slid into her hair, curving around the back of her neck. "If I agree with that, will you stop beating yourself up about it?" His voice was so kind.

Against her will, her gaze dipped, slid over him, his broad shoulders, sculpted chest, narrow hips. She looked back at his face. "Maybe."

"Then I agree. It was just sex." He nodded, encouraging her to agree, too.

She nodded along with him. "Good sex." She swallowed, her mouth suddenly dry. Damn. It was starting again. The wanting. "But just sex."

"Great sex, in fact. But still just sex."

The heat was building again and she started to turn away.

"Chass, wait, my—"

But she couldn't wait. She couldn't let him see the reawakened hunger in her eyes. As she pivoted, she felt a tug behind her neck and the black triangles of fabric fell away from her breasts.

"Fingers are caught," he finished, before the power of speech deserted him. They both stilled. Gabe sucked in a breath, suddenly needing the oxygen. "Perfect," he said quietly, awed by the sight of her.

Slowly, he disentangled his fingers from the thin straps. He watched her face as he slid his hand forward, his fingers traveling slowly downward till he cupped one soft, rounded breast in his palm. He lifted his other hand to do the same and brushed his thumbs over her nipples.

Hunger burned in her eyes. Her lips parted, but it was several seconds before she spoke. "Don't," she said, but the word came out breathy, and she leaned into his touch.

Gabe swallowed. "Do you really mean 'don't'?

Because if you do, I need to know now." She didn't say anything, gave just the smallest sideways movement of her head. Slowly, he lowered his head, took one peaked nipple in his mouth, and teased it with his tongue.

"That's not fair," she whispered, arching into him.

Reluctantly he gave up the exquisite pleasure of her nipple, but he didn't seem able to keep his lips, or his hands, off her. This time he kissed her mouth as he slid his arms around her, bare skin against still-damp bare skin. She was so slender, she should have felt vulnerable within the circle of his arms, and yet the power of her need radiated from her.

She pressed against him and he was lost. He drank in the sweet taste of her, tried to keep control of the kiss, tried to keep at least a portion of his brain functioning. He gripped her hips, fingertips pressing into the softness of her behind. Did she have any idea what she did to him? He broke the kiss and tucked a strand of damp hair behind her ear.

"You're not fair. I have no strength, no defense against your beauty, your perfection. You are my every fantasy."

Chastity opened her mouth to say something, but no words came out. She licked her lips, about to try again, but Gabe bent and scooped her into his arms. He held her gaze, let her see his hunger.

In three steps he'd laid her down on the bed and sat beside her. She reached for him, but he encircled her wrists with his fingers and raised her arms up above her head. With his other hand he drew her top away, tossed it to the floor. Her bikini bottoms followed. "Beautiful," he said on a rough sigh. She was laid bare for him, and he was honored. This woman was so many things he was just beginning to guess at.

He looked into her eyes as, starting at her hairline, he trailed his fingers down the side of her face, her jaw, along her throat and through the dip between her collarbones that, against all reason, he considered his. Heat bloomed in her cheeks as he moved his hand lower, over the swell of her breast and the straining nipple. Her eyes darkened as he traced the outline of her ribs, the curve of her waist, the flare of her hips.

He slid his palm across to rest on the gentle swell of her abdomen.

His child grew within her.

The rush of protectiveness and possessiveness that knowledge caused stunned him with its ferocity.

"Gabe." She whispered her need through parted lips, a whisper that spoke directly to the answering need in him.

He brought his hand to rest at the apex of her thighs, covering the blond curls. With his fingers he parted her folds, found her slick and hot. She rose up and opened to him.

"Please." She sounded as desperate as he felt. "I need you inside me."

He slid fingers inside her tightness.

"But you?" she said, puzzled.

"This one is just for you." With his thumb, he explored till he found the spot that made her gasp. And then he pleasured her, felt the fierceness of her desire building ever higher, till she was writhing and gasping. He covered her mouth with his, tasting her ecstasy as she climaxed, her hips rising up, her muscles convulsing around his fingers.

They were both breathing hard as she sank back into the bed. He let go of her hands and she clung to him. The early morning peace settled over them, and despite his own need for release, Gabe felt a contentment he hadn't expected, a pleasure in just knowing he had given her pleasure. Somehow it meant more than anything he could remember.

And then she was moving again. She insinuated herself more completely beneath him. Her hands tugged at the waistband of his trunks and he took the hint, shucking them before settling himself between her thighs.

Her hand found him more than ready. She stroked his length as she guided him home. He paused at her entrance. She raised her hips to him, wrapped her long legs around him. He slid in, slowly, exquisitely slowly, sheathing himself in her.

Chastity smiled. "This one's for you."

Just as slowly he pulled out—almost completely—before sliding in again. He repeated the movement again, watching her.

Her smile disappeared and she frowned. "Don't expect me to... I won't be able to... Not so soon."

It was Gabe's turn to smile. "I don't expect anything of you," he said as he kept moving within her, his rhythm building.

Chastity's frown turned to confusion and then surprise.

He plunged deeper, faster, into her heat, watched her eyes darken. He slid a hand between them, found the same spot he had earlier, saw its immediate effect, heard it in her ragged breathing.

They were moving together, a powerful physical joining.

And something more than just physical.

The blood roared in his ears as he watched the need and passion overtake her. He thought for a moment that she resisted it before giving in. And as her climax took her, he exploded into her.

Gabe could hear Chastity in the bathroom—quietly crying. That wasn't the effect he usually had on women. He hesitated outside the bathroom door. If he called to her, asked if he could come in, she'd only tell him to go away. So he opened the door, thankful that the locks hadn't yet been fitted and walked in.

Chastity sat in a corner, wearing a bathrobe, hugging the knees pulled up to her chest. The sight cut a hole in his chest.

"Go away. It's nothing. Sometimes I just need to cry." She turned her head so that her still damp hair curtained her face.

He sat down beside her.

She wiped at her eyes with the sleeve of her bathrobe. "What part of 'go away' don't you understand?"

He slid his arm behind her back. "Don't cry, Chass. What's wrong? Did I hurt you?"

She leaned in to him, pressed her forehead to his shoulder. "Don't worry, it's not you." She sniffed. "Well, not what you think."

"What do you mean?"

"Nothing. Just go away."

"I'm not going away and leaving you like this."

"I'm fine. Really. It just looks bad."

"You're right about that. It looks bad. Really. I'd have to say you're not fine."

"But I am. That's why I'm crying."

"This is woman's logic, isn't it?"

She gave a hiccuping laugh that did little to ease the bands tightening his chest.

"Why did it have to be you? No one's ever...done that to me before."

He stiffened, thought back over their morning. "Oh, God. You weren't a—"

This time she laughed properly. "No. I wasn't a virgin."

"Then what did you mean? No one's ever..."

She buried her face in her knees. "Made it good for me. Like that. Like you did. Took time for...me."

Something burned within him. Why hadn't she been treasured? "Who've you been sleeping with?"

"No one, actually. Not for a long time. Like I said, I thought it was overrated."

Did she still think that? He wasn't going to ask the question. His masculine pride was not important right now.

She turned her head, resting her cheek on her knees so she could look at him. The sweetest smile played about her lips, her blue eyes sparkled. "I don't think it's overrated anymore. I can kind of see what the fuss is about. Although I'm not sure if that's you or just pregnancy hormones."

Again he said nothing, though the effort cost him.

"I only ever slept with one other guy."

"One?"

"My swim coach in college."

"Wasn't that unethical? Of him," he added quickly.

"Yes. It was. He was good-looking, he'd been an Olympic swimmer himself. It was all so cliché. I thought he cared. Turns out so did two other girls on the team. That I knew of."

"Did you do anything about it? Did anything happen to him or did he get away with it?"

"One of the other girls, Monica, was much stronger, and more bitter, than me. I was just…humiliated. She took it higher."

"And what happened?"

"I don't know."

"What do you mean?"

"I left school and came back to New Zealand."

He pulled her closer to him. Wished he could undo the last few hours, have them over again. One guy? She'd only ever slept with one other guy and he'd been a self-centered louse. She deserved the magic, not the insatiable hunger that had driven him. She deserved dinners and flowers and romance. He could give her that, at least.

A uniformed crew member handed Chastity up onto the yacht, nodded as Gabe spoke quietly to him, and then disappeared into the night. Chastity looked around in awe. How did something this big, with not a sail in sight, come to be called a yacht? Her survey took in the darkening water, the stars that were starting to appear in the sky, then the gleaming handrails and fittings of the yacht. She smoothed her hands over her white linen pants, adjusted her turquoise halter-neck top. She looked anywhere but at the man beside her. His subtle scent, almost like that of the ocean itself, and his very nearness invaded her senses.

She'd spent another day in his company. He'd left his phone behind. Voluntarily. Another day of nothing and yet everything. They'd forgotten about the past and the future and had a day of moments, of nows. Created memories Chastity knew she'd treasure once this was over.

Apart from the lap of water against the hull of the yacht, all about them was still and quiet. Finally she looked at Gabe, who she'd known was watching her. He stood casually, hands loose at his sides, a single step away. His dark eyes held hers.

She saw the dark hair, the strong jaw, the eminently kissable lips and the broad shoulders. And she'd seen so very much more. The perfect whole. Yet she hadn't the faintest idea what was going on beneath his enigmatic appraisal. So much had changed between them, for her at least.

A second crew member materialized, wearing the same white shirt and long white pants as the first. With a friendly smile to her and a respectful nod at Gabe, he led them to the dining area. Candles flickered on a table laid with a linen cloth and set with gleaming silver cutlery for two. The scent of roses from an enormous white bouquet perfumed the air. Soft, smoky jazz played from unseen speakers. As a low rumble vibrated through the boat, the man who'd led them here pulled out a chair for Chastity. After he'd seated both her and Gabe, he, too, disappeared.

"So, this seems awfully like a—"

"Date. Yes." Gabe smiled.

"Why?" He wasn't known for his spontaneity. He was a calculator, a planner. She couldn't help but be anxious that his calculations and plans were suddenly including her. Now seemed like a very good time to start worrying. "I'm not going to sleep with you again," she jumped in before he could even answer. "You're wasting your efforts and both of our time if that's where you think this is going." He studied her. Waiting. "Because that was a monumental mistake. I'm not saying it wasn't... Well, I'm not saying anything aside from the fact that it was a mistake. Which you have to know, too. So now I'll shut up because clearly I'm babbling, which I do when I'm nervous. But you can talk and you can tell me why you think we're here."

Chastity clamped her lips together and silence fell. Gabe waited a couple of beats, all the while watching her with that unwavering, unnerving gaze. "It's not because I want to sleep with you again. Which I'll concede wasn't the wisest thing we could have done. And if that—" he continued—but at his emphasis on the word *that* and the subtle darkening of his gaze, Chastity felt her traitorous body respond "—was what I wanted, or thought you wanted, this isn't where we'd be right now." And that was all it took for her mind to flash back to tangled sheets and tangled limbs and Gabe over her and inside her.

She recalled, though she'd forbidden herself from recalling it, how very, very good it—he—had been. How physically he'd intuited so much about her, almost more than she herself knew, and then used it—with her consent, if you called pleading consent—to overwhelm her, carry her to places of fantasy.

She swallowed, looked down and realigned her cutlery.

He touched the back of her hands with his fingertips. A fleeting…caress. "And I don't mean to make you nervous."

She regretted that particular admission of weakness. Gabe was of the "knowledge is power" school and she'd just given him power. It was time to claim some back for herself. Folding her arms, she lifted her chin. "Then why are we here?" She was prepared to confront him. She wasn't prepared for the melting gentleness in his brown eyes.

A waiter appeared and set bowls of aromatic soup in front of them and a basket of assorted breads between them. When he'd withdrawn from the room Gabe spoke. "Because everything has happened backward. Pregnant first, sex second." He held her gaze and it was all she could do not to look away in embarrassment. How was it that he could be so seemingly blasé about…that? He had rocked her world. "A date seemed like the next logical step."

The next logical step. So he did have a plan, or was at least formulating one. It was time to be worried. Time to shore up her own defenses. Because there was a warning voice in her head shouting at her to watch her step, and even to watch her heart, that if Gabe decided to be charming, she was history. She'd already shown him far too much about herself. She reached for a chunk of bread. "Maybe we don't need to get to know each other. Maybe we just need to figure out—when it becomes necessary—how we're going to manage your contact with my daughter."

"Our daughter." He spoke calmly, quietly.

"My. Daughter."

"You're going to try to deny that she's mine?" Still calm, almost quizzical.

"Not biologically. And not in private."

"But legally?"

"It's not about me denying it. It's about you being clear on precisely what the letter of the law is."

"But we're not talking about the letter of the law, are we? It's never that clear-cut when people and emotions are involved."

"No," she said on a sigh. "I know." And that was where the problems lay. Her emotions where this man was concerned. The fact that he might be a good father. In fact, there was no *might* about it. If it was what he wanted, as he said he did, he would be a very good father. If he accepted, as he seemed to, that it was worth spending less time immersed in his all-consuming work to spend time with a child, her daughter, then her little girl would be one very lucky child. Because he was so good at everything he did. And beneath the Granite Man exterior, beneath the strategist, lay someone gentle and loving and strong.

Chastity turned her attention to her soup. It was the only thing that wasn't confusing her. After a couple of delicious mouthfuls she looked back up at him, so calm, so patient, so sure of himself. And she wanted to be angry at him, or to at least find something that would level the playing field, give her a sense of power. "Is there anything you're not good at? Do you have any failures in life?"

"Yes."

"What?"

He took a deep breath. "My relationship with Tom."

She set her spoon down. Of course. Tom who'd gotten them into this mess. Tom whose relationship with his family had broken down almost completely, as he'd wanted it to, from the moment Chastity moved into his apartment.

"Was he gay?"

She broke a chunk of bread in two, keeping her focus fixed on it. "You can't ask me that."

"I just did."

"He was *your* brother."

"And now he's dead, so I can't ask him."

She sometimes forgot that Gabe had suffered the same loss as her, the loss of Tom. From what she knew, they hadn't had a great relationship, especially in later years, but a brother was a brother and death was forever. "Then don't worry about it because it doesn't make any difference, does it? It can't bring him back."

"But it would explain so much." She saw the puzzlement in his eyes. Gabe with all the answers didn't know what he needed to figure this one out. "We were close once. And then it all changed. It started well before you came on the scene. Probably in his late teens. A distance came between us. He became more and more secretive about his private life. I asked him once, outright."

"And?" Tom had never told her this. He'd said his family didn't have a clue, but that it was willful ignorance because knowing would destroy them.

"He bloodied my nose for it."

"Really?" She almost smiled. Tom would have been secretly both shocked and proud of himself.

"Only because he caught me by surprise."

"Naturally."

Gabe grinned. Then the lift of his lips disappeared. "I never asked again. I figured if he was, he'd tell me if and when he was ready. Then later he took up with you and I thought, okay, definitely not gay. Now the envy of every red-blooded male he knows. But through eighteen months of engagement and six months of marriage you never slept together. And it's the only explanation I can think of."

"It is possible for people to wait."

"It wouldn't be possible for me if I was going to marry you. Not unless I could arrange a same-day marriage."

"Is that a backhanded compliment or an insult? No, don't answer that, this conversation's not about me. I don't care."

"How could it possibly be an insult?"

"As in clearly that would be the only real reason for marrying someone like me, nothing worth waiting for, nothing worth celebrating. Step up to some hole-in-the-wall place, that'll be fine."

"How can you think so little of yourself?"

"I don't. But I'm more than used to it in others."

"If I loved someone enough to marry them, I wouldn't want to wait for any of it. I would want the world to know she was the woman I'd chosen and that she'd chosen me back. I'd want her to take my name. I'd want to share it all, with her as my life's partner. Sunrises, sunsets and everything in between. The walking, the talking, the moments of stillness and, yes, the making love."

She saw the passion and intensity in his eyes, heard it in his words. And it made her feel almost sorry for herself. She didn't know that she'd ever find the sort of love Gabe would one day offer. "She'll be a lucky woman. The woman who marries you."

"And he'll be a lucky man. The man who captures your heart."

"Let's hope he thinks so." She looked out the window to a night that revealed nothing.

Firm fingers touched her jaw, turned her face back to him. "He couldn't possibly think otherwise." His eyes. Did he know he had the kindest eyes? The sexiest, kindest eyes.

Those warm, sure fingers stayed on her skin for several beats before he lowered his hand to the table, clenched it around his knife and turned his attention to spreading pesto on a chunk of bread. "So, Tom was gay?"

"It's not for me to tell you one way or another."

"He was gay." Gabe chewed a piece of perfectly cooked fillet steak. "I just can't believe I ever doubted it. And I can't believe he didn't trust me enough to tell me."

"The perfect Gabe? He was going to reveal what he considered, and what he knew your family considered, such a flaw, to you, the Golden Boy?"

Gabe looked at her. And she realized she'd as good as told him what she'd vowed to herself she wouldn't.

Gabe sat back and for a minute looked into the distance. He was somewhere else altogether. Then, abruptly he leaned forward in his seat. "I get why Tom did it. It was an elaborate sham. You were his smoke screen. But why were you with him? Why even agree in the first place to the pretense of an engagement?" His gaze had changed, was now assessing, intent. There was no lingering sadness or softness, just a determination to get answers. "You must have had reasons. More than I initially thought."

Chastity put her hands flat on the table. "Why the in-quisition when this is supposed to be a date?"

Gabe was about to respond, to counter, she was guessing, when the waiter appeared. When he'd gone Gabe spoke quietly. "Sorry. You're right." But the as-sessment was still there in his eyes. She didn't know what he was thinking, but whatever it was unnerved her. "At one time I thought you might have had feelings for me."

So he had known. "I did," she admitted because there was no point denying it.

He frowned. "Then, why Tom?"

"You transferred me. I thought you'd figured out that I was attracted to you and that you didn't want... that. Me."

Gabe leaned forward, his stare intense. "You didn't think that maybe I transferred you precisely because I did want you? But because I was such a staunch and vocal advocate against relationships between people who worked closely together within the company, that I wanted to put some distance between us first?"

"No." She'd never in her wildest dreams thought that. Gabe's rejection, which is what she'd viewed it as, had seemed perfectly reasonable for someone like him.

"Beneath it all, I was jealous of Tom. That's why I allowed the distance between us to grow."

"I never thought."

"No. Perhaps neither of us thought things through properly."

As much as she wanted to believe that things might have been different, a relationship with Gabe couldn't have lasted. Tom understood about secrets and imperfections. He let her keep her secrets just as she let him keep his. Neither of them pried into the other's life. Gabe would never accept something that superficial.

"I still don't understand why you two suddenly decided to get married and have a child though."

Chastity was quiet a moment. "It was after my grandmother died that we got to talking about it. Tom wanted the appearance of a real family and he said he wanted an heir. And I wanted…someone to love. I wanted a real family, too, I guess. And I didn't want to have a baby outside of marriage."

A tear leaked from her eye and she wiped it away. "This wasn't a good idea. Can we go back to shore? I'm tired." She was tired of trying to figure out where she was with him. There were too many layers. There was Gabe the man she'd made love with, Gabe the father of her child, Gabe the brother of the man she'd married. And they were all layered together in the man sitting opposite her, watching her. It was too much to keep straight in her head.

"Let's finish eating. Adam prepared the menu specifically for you."

"He's here?"

"No. The yacht has its own chef, but Adam planned the menu."

"Oh." She had no friend here to shield her from Gabe. Though thinking Adam could help, when it was her own feelings that were the problem, was futile. She squared her shoulders. This was for her and her alone to deal with. "Okay. But no more questions?"

"No more questions. And then afterward, there's one thing I'd like to show you."

"I don't know." She should get away. She was spending far too much time with him and it was confusing her in so many ways.

"I think you'll like it. And there's nothing devious, no ulterior motive in it." He held his hands out, palms toward her.

"It won't take long? Because I really am tired." Tired of trying not to be beguiled by him.

"No."

"Okay then."

He smiled, a gentle approving smile that coaxed one in return from her. Far too beguiling. She had to turn away from the warmth in his eyes before it kindled back to flame the embers of desire that had taken up permanent residence within her.

Ten

They stood together at the railing, a careful distance between them, as the boat motored through the water. "What is it I'm supposed to be looking at?" she asked. Dusk had bled into night. But the moon again hung unobscured and bright in the sky.

"Just wait. You can't see it yet."

"How long? Because soon I'll scarcely be able to see anything at all."

"I can't say. Maybe a few more minutes, maybe longer. Just wait."

"But—"

He quieted her with a hand on her shoulder. "Soon. I promise. Or we'll go back to shore."

"Can't you at least tell me what I'm looking for?"

"No. Watch the water."

His hand tightened, but before he could say anything,

she saw it. A flash of glistening silver-gray curved in the water where there should have been nothing. And then another. "Gabe. Was that—"

"Just watch."

Suddenly several dolphins broke the water, leaping and diving in graceful arcs through the yacht's wake. Then up ahead first one and then another leaped into the air, seeming to stand for an instant on their tails before dropping back down. A mother and young dolphin played together at the edge of the pod. For ten minutes Chastity watched in awed silence as the pod performed— because it felt like a performance—for them. And then just as suddenly as they'd appeared, they were gone. And she was leaning back in Gabe's arms stunned by the beauty and privilege of what they'd just seen.

For long minutes more they just stood there. She didn't want to move. Didn't want to break the magic of what they'd experienced or the subtler magic of leaning into Gabe's strength, of having his arms around her.

Later as they stood on the jetty, the big yacht's tender heading back out, she turned to Gabe, whose hand she still held from when he'd helped her off the boat, whose hand she couldn't quite bring herself to let go of. Yet. "Thank you."

"You liked it?"

"It was amazing. I've never seen anything so beautiful." She'd moved closer to him so they were separated by only a whisper of air.

He threaded his fingers through her hair, a thumb pressed gently against her jaw. His eyes searched her face. "I have."

Slowly, he lowered his head. She could have stopped the kiss if she'd wanted to. But the very last thing in the world she wanted was to stop his kiss. As his mouth covered hers with an aching tenderness, she melted against him. She forgot every one of the multitude of reasons why she shouldn't be doing this and clung to him instead—the one real, solid thing in her universe. He tasted of the coffee they'd finished dinner with. His hint of stubble abraded her palms as she touched his face, slid her hands into his hair. She tried to let this be enough. This one consuming kiss that fired her senses. But it held the promise of so much more.

She pulled away from him. "We shouldn't."

"No. We shouldn't."

He lowered his head again, tasted her, savored her once more.

He held her to him and she felt the passion vibrating through him, an echo of her own pulsing need.

He lifted his head. "So, I'll just walk you back to your chalet."

Chastity nodded, mute.

Neither of them moved, till finally, her hand, of its own volition, lifted and her fingertips grazed over his chest. Still ignoring the protest of what remained of her sanity, they shifted and flicked the fabric from around the first button, and then the second and third so that she could slide her palm inside his shirt and rest it on the warm skin there, feel the beat of his heart beneath her touch.

She looked up from what she was doing and into his eyes. If onlys—her mind teemed with them. If only she'd met someone like Gabe earlier in her life. If only she'd met…Gabe. There was no someone else like him, there was only him. And she was in deep, deep trouble.

She could never have him. He didn't want a woman like her. Warm fingertips traced the shape of her collarbone. Well, he might want her now. But not permanently. Not in the way she was realizing she wanted him.

His lips found hers.

He deserved someone from his own background. Someone he could make a life with. Someone who wasn't faking that she could belong in the strata he lived in.

She had to leave before she was hopelessly lost. His kiss deepened. And she knew she was too late to stop losing herself. Live in the moment. Wasn't that what she'd told him to do?

She would take tonight. What was one more night of passion between them? She took hold of his hands. "Your chalet. It's closer." His hands cupped her jaw as he searched her face. She could only hope that in her eyes the desire overrode the love.

Chastity was dreaming of drums when something woke her. Lying on her back, she stretched out alongside Gabe and allowed herself a moment to savor the sensation, the bliss and contentment of his warmth and nearness, his subtle male scent. There was surely no better place in the world to wake. She opened her eyes to find Gabe lifted up on one elbow, a lock of his hair falling forward, brown eyes studying her, and the softest of smiles playing about his lips. Morning sunlight streamed in through the window behind her, bathing him in gold.

He touched his fingers to her stomach. "It's a good

thing you were already pregnant, because if you weren't, you surely would have been by now." His smile widened. His gaze full of tenderness.

An ache bloomed in her heart. Was there a way they could make this work? Could she make him love her? Could they have a future?

Two quick raps sounded on the door before it swung open. Gabe's body blocked her line of sight. "Gabe," the high, cultured voice cut through the air and Chastity tensed. She didn't need a line of sight to recognize his mother.

Not drums—a helicopter.

She tried to shrink down beneath the sheet, but Gabe's touch, his fingers in her hair, stilled her, his calm gaze locked on hers, held her where she was, promised that everything would be okay. For long seconds he stayed just like that, then with a caress of her cheek he slowly turned, still shielding her with his body. "I really have to do something about getting locks fitted."

"Gabe, your father and I were worried. No one's been able to reach you for two days. And after Tom…" Chastity heard the tension in Cynthia's voice and then the slow, ominous tap of her footsteps as she came farther into the room. One more step and Chastity could see her, see the worry in her eyes. Guilt bloomed. She hadn't been thinking of his family when she'd taken his phone. She'd forgotten how an inability to reach Tom had been the first sign that anything was amiss.

"And," Cynthia continued, "Marco's going crazy. The Turner deal is floundering. He's had to bring the Tokyo delegation—" Her gaze finally lighted on Chastity, and worry turned to horror. "What is that…slut doing here?"

Chastity shrank back at the venom of her words as Gabe swung himself to sitting, still shielding her with his body and keeping the sheet both over her and his hips. "Do not *ever* call her that again."

For a moment, Cynthia looked taken aback at Gabe's vehemence, but she rallied instantly. "I speak as I find. As I know."

"You're wrong."

"You're telling me that you didn't just sleep with her? Let me guess, you didn't finish *talking* the other night she stayed with you? And you needed to be naked and in your bed to have the rest of the conversation?"

Gabe folded his arms across his chest. "I'm not telling you anything that's none of your business."

"By my definition, sleeping with another of my sons only months after burying the first, the one she was married to, qualifies as a—"

"It's not how it looks."

"You mean walking in here and finding that—"

"Cynthia," he cut her off again before she could call Chastity anything else. "Go to the restaurant. I'll come talk to you there."

Cynthia's face was tight-lipped and livid with fury as she sucked in a breath through her nose. She pointed a manicured finger at Chastity. "Leave my son alone. You've cost me one already. You're not getting your conniving, money-grubbing hands on another."

"Cynthia—"

But Cynthia had turned and gone.

He turned to Chastity. "I'm sorry about that."

"It's okay."

"It's not okay." He reached for a strand of her hair,

ran it through his fingers. "And I really am sorry. She shouldn't have said that. When she understands what's really going on—"

"There's no need to apologize. It doesn't matter to me what your mother thinks."

His gaze held hers. "I'd be happier if I believed that." He ran a gentle knuckle along her jaw.

"Then believe it." She slithered past him and out of the bed, pulled on her underwear, picked up her bra from the floor. As she struggled with its catch, Gabe, who'd managed to get at least half-dressed too, came to stand behind her, shifted her fumbling hands away and did it up.

With his hands on her shoulders, he turned her. "I can't believe it when it's clearly not the truth."

Chastity stared at the smooth muscle of his shoulder and tried to find the right words to convince him.

"Come with me to talk to her."

She swung out of his grip and lunged for her linen pants and stepped into them. "Not if my life depended on it."

"Why not? If you don't care what she thinks, it shouldn't make any difference."

She pulled her top over her head. "Because she's right. I was married to Tom." She crossed her arms, holding on to her shoulders.

Gently, Gabe uncrossed them, his hands holding her wrists. "It wasn't a real marriage though, was it?"

She shook her head.

"You've slept with a grand total of two men. The first, a guy in a position of authority over you who you thought you loved, and the second whose child you're already carrying and who took advantage of a moment of weakness. Well, several moments of weakness. But who's counting?"

Chastity smiled. "That's very chivalrous of you, but we both know that if anyone was taking advantage, it wasn't you."

"Stop trying to take the blame or I'll take advantage of you again, right here and right now just to prove my point."

Chastity tried to take a step back, but he still had her wrists and instead of releasing them, stepped up to her. She caught, and recognized, the look in his eyes as he lowered his head. She turned her face so that his kiss landed on the corner of her lips. So gentle. He shifted so that his next kiss connected properly and he coaxed her lips apart. Chastity leaned into the kiss, into Gabe, as his arms slipped around her, holding her to him. His kiss held the sweetest tenderness and longing. She softened against him, wanted to meld herself to him, wanted to stay like this forever, loving Gabe.

Chastity pushed herself away. Loving Gabe? Please, no.

Gabe blinked and studied her. "See what I mean? That, Chastity, was me taking advantage of you. Not the other way around. Now, I'm going to talk to my mother before she has a coronary. Are you coming?"

Chastity shook her head. She couldn't love Gabe. She wouldn't let herself. Loving Gabe would only mean pain and heartbreak.

"Don't look so terrified. She can be a drama queen, but she doesn't know you. She's never had the chance. If she did…"

And if only he knew why she was really looking terrified. She tried to focus on the conversation Gabe thought they were having. "She'd what? See a gold digger trying to trap another of her sons."

"She'd see an incredibly strong woman who's true to herself and who's made something of herself against the odds. A woman with a kind, loving heart."

If only he knew just how loving. If only he knew that her loving heart had given itself to him. He'd be in the water and swimming for the mainland. Or worse, laughing pityingly at her.

"Go and see her. She needs you."

"What about you? Do you need me here? I'll stay if you do."

She couldn't stop the leap of her heart at his question even though she knew he was talking about the present moment only. "No. Go. You're her only son now. She's hurting."

"Wait for me. I'll be back soon."

Chastity watched him leave and felt the tears well and then trickle down her face. It was over. All good things must come to an end. Wasn't that how the saying went? She'd had her days—and nights—of perfection. But Gabe would come to his senses. Pick up the mantle of responsibility again. Which is exactly what he should do. And the fact that he would was part of why she loved him.

He was going back to the world he belonged in. A world she couldn't be a part of. She'd been able to make a life with Tom because Tom, rightly or wrongly, had believed he needed to be apart from his family. But Gabe and his mother and father were all each other had now and she knew what it was like to lose the last of

your family. She couldn't come between them. Even if
Gabe wanted her.

She stared out the window, watched him stride toward the restaurant. The words needed to escape her and
make themselves heard. Just once. "I love you." He
paused and looked back, though he couldn't possibly
have heard her. Then he kept right on walking.

Chastity rested her forehead against the glass. Of all
the stupid things she could have done.

Gabe set a cup of coffee down in front of Cynthia.
"So, what's the problem with the Turner deal? What's
Marco doing with the Tokyo delegation?"

His mother's hands clenched into fists on the table.
"You think I can talk about the Turner deal after what I
just saw, knowing that woman's here? With you?"

She had a point there. Gabe, too, didn't want to talk or
even think about the Turner deal, knowing that Chastity
was here and probably now in her chalet fretting, blaming
herself. "Her name's Chastity and we're not going to have
any kind of conversation unless you can remember that."

"I can remember that. Can you remember that she
ensnared your brother, cost him his family?"

Gabe looked at his mother. She excelled at laying
blame at other people's doors. And far too often she got
away with it. "Maybe we cost him his family. Maybe
Chastity was a convenient excuse for cutting himself off
and not the real reason."

His mother stared in horror. "She's poisoned you,
too, hasn't she?" Sniffing, she reached for her handbag
and started rummaging for a tissue. It was an act though.
She wouldn't cry; it would ruin her makeup.

"No. But I've learned some things about myself and about Tom from Chastity. Things I should have seen a long time ago."

Cynthia pulled out a tissue and dabbed at her eyes. "What sort of things?"

His mother wasn't going to take this well, but it was time his family stopped hiding from their secrets before what little remained of it self-destructed. "Where's Dad?" If he had to break this news to his mother then he may as well tell both parents at once, and Cynthia would need his father here, too.

"Playing golf. Where else would he be? These days it's all he ever—never mind." The tissue disappeared within her fist. "Why, Gabe? Tell me why that woman's here. What sort of hold has she got over you?"

Maybe his mother was partially right. Chastity did have some kind of hold over him. But it was the very best kind of hold. And he was suddenly hoping that their days here had been enough to give him the same kind of hold over her. The very best kind. He quelled the smile that threatened before his mother could see it.

If Chastity was here with him now, he could admit that to her and they could tell Cynthia about the baby— their baby. Once his mother accepted that news it would do her good, give her something positive in her life to look forward to. But Chastity wasn't here. And he wasn't telling his mother without her permission.

"I can see why you might be attracted to her. She's a beautiful woman. But there's no shortage of beautiful women."

"Not like her."

Cynthia's mouth dropped open at his defense of

Chastity. Her eyes blazed with a bitterness he hated to see there. "She's nothing more than a gold digger. You've said it yourself in the past. Have you forgotten that? Is she really that good in—"

Gabe held up a hand to stop her words, and he frowned.

She was no gold digger. She didn't seem to care at all about money. She loved the beach and wore shell jewelry made by a child. She cared about others. She protected those she cared about, took the blame for things like seduction when it didn't belong to her. And she was everything he wanted in a woman and more. She was more than he deserved.

He thought about the hours he'd spent making love with Chastity. Chastity, who was kind and loving and passionate and vulnerable. And he remembered, too, that time two years ago that she had first touched his heart as they'd sat in the sunlight on a river bank. He thought of their walks along the beach, of her delight in the simplest things in life, of the wonder in her eyes as she'd watched the dolphins. It was, he realized, just last night, as they'd stood on the deck of the yacht and he'd been watching her rather than the dolphins, that everything had come together for him, the physical and the emotional becoming something more. It was then that everything had changed irrevocably.

He loved her.

Completely and utterly. He wanted to share his life with her; he wanted to share hers. She was the woman he wanted to walk along the sand with, swinging their child between them. Her and no one else.

"We had her investigated, you know," Cynthia finally said when he didn't respond.

"You did what?" he asked, still processing his re-alization. He loved Chastity Stevens. He wanted her to be Chastity Masters, to take his name and be his wife in all the ways she'd never been Tom's.

"When she moved in with Tom, your father and I had her investigated."

Gabe stood up. "How dare you?"

"She's completely unsuitable." Cynthia clearly failed to comprehend his outrage. "We tried to tell Tom, but he wouldn't listen. Her family, if you can call it a family, is trash, perfectly revolting. Her mother was an alco-holic and died of cirrhosis of the liver, but was known as the town slut. Her half sisters, from different fathers, I might add, are no better."

Gabe turned on his heel.

"Where are you going?" Cynthia's voice climbed several notches.

"To Chastity."

"Don't you dare walk away from me for her."

Gabe stepped out of the restaurant in time to see the mail ferry tied up at the jetty and Marco leading a party of dark-haired and dark-suited businessmen toward him. His heart sank. He had a few scant seconds to look in the direction of the chalets, seeing nothing and no one, before the men were upon him.

"I couldn't get in touch with you. We had to rearrange the schedule, and they wanted to meet with you person-ally," Marco said quietly as they approached. "As far as they're concerned, *you* are Masters' Developments." Gabe accepted the explanation with a nod. He knew the importance of perceived status and personal relation-ships. "And," Marco continued, "they want to see what's going on here first." The Turner deal, a joint venture in conjunction with the men now in front of him, would be their biggest yet. Three linked resorts on three Pacific islands.

And then the formalities began. The greetings of those he already knew, the introductions to those he didn't, the presentation of business cards. Gabe tried to focus.

"We'll need to arrange some kind of entertainment for this afternoon," Marco suggested just a short while later as they were touring the resort's facilities. "They've also been seeing Jacobs. He's trying to woo them."

"I'll call Julia, get her to organize a big-game fishing expedition." He looked up and saw his mother walking toward the restaurant—from the direction of Chastity's chalet. His gaze lighted on a solitary figure making her way down the jetty, hauling a too-heavy suitcase.

Eleven

He turned back to Marco. "You handle this. I have to go."

Marco followed his gaze. "You can't seriously be thinking about leaving this for her?"

"Apparently I can."

"Are you crazy? They're already jittery. If you leave now, the deal will fall through. You know how touchy they can be. And there's nothing more important to us right now than this."

The low rumble of the ferry's engines carried to him. "Maybe I am crazy, but there is something, *someone,* more important than this. And I'm not going to lose her for the sake of a few million. You handle it. It's what you do." He turned to the delegation. "Excuse me, gentlemen. Please accept my sincere apologies."

And then he was sprinting for the jetty.

He made it onto the ferry with a leap that barely cleared

the rapidly widening gap of water. On deck, he pulled out his cell phone and called his PA. "Julia, forget about whatever else you have planned for today. I have something you need to organize. Bring in any and all help you need. Pull out all the stops." He talked to her for a few minutes longer then made his way to the bow of the boat, eased alongside the woman facing forward, her tousled hair blowing in the breeze. Their shoulders touched and she stiffened.

"The helicopter's faster," he said. "The ferry has to stop at several more islands farther out before heading back for the mainland. It'll be a few hours still."

"The ferry was leaving sooner." Her hands were clenched around the railing.

"Ahh."

"Shouldn't you be back on the island?"

She still hadn't looked at him and he studied her profile, her pale, perfect profile. "Perhaps that's where I *should* be. But I'm precisely where I want to be."

She slid the briefest, concerned glance at him and he saw the redness of her eyes, and the pinkened end of her nose.

"Am I right in thinking you've had the pleasure of a chat with my mother?"

"Pleasure's probably not the word I'd use."

"No. I don't suppose it would be. So, what did she say?"

Chastity said nothing.

"Let me guess. She ranted for a while and when that didn't achieve what she wanted, when she figured out that you had…feelings." He watched her stiffen. "Real feelings for me, she changed her tack. Said that a relationship with you would harm my standing in the business community, make me a laughingstock. She said that you would cost me my family. That if you really loved me, you'd walk away."

"You've pretty much nailed it."

"And do you? Love me?"

"No." She kept her focus firmly fixed on the wide ocean, but he heard the catch in her voice and his heart swelled.

"You really are a terrible liar."

She pressed her lips together.

"I think you do love me."

"It doesn't have to mean anything."

"It means everything. To me." The ferry pushed through a wave and Gabe put his arm around Chastity, pulled her closer to him. "So, back to my mother."

"She's lost so much."

"She's not the only one."

"I told her that I would leave you…alone. I mean, it's not like we even had a real relationship."

"No."

Chastity smiled sadly. "She can be very gracious when she's getting her own way."

"And I can be very pigheaded until I get mine."

She slid a glance at him, a frown marring her brow.

He turned her toward him and pushed a strand of hair behind her ear, then left his palm resting against her cheek. For a moment she leaned into his touch. "Did I mention that I loved you, too?"

Tears welled in her eyes. "Don't, Gabe." She tried to turn away.

His lifted his other hand so that he cradled her face

between his palms. "Don't what?" He held her gaze. "Tell you that I love you?"

She closed her eyes. "Yes. That."

"But I do," he said quietly. "Nothing about you is how I'd convinced myself you were. But I had to do that. Because if I'd let myself see who you really were, I would have wanted you too badly for myself."

"That's just it. You don't know who I really am."

"I do."

"No. About my family. My mother. My sisters."

"I don't care."

"Only because you don't know."

"No. I do not care. The only thing, the only *one* I care about is you."

"Your mother cares. She knows about my family. And your parents have already lost one son. They're hurting. I won't cost them another."

"And what about you? What about me? My hurt. Do I have to lose Tom and now you, too?"

"When you're ready, you'll find someone. The right kind of woman for you."

"Right for me or right for my mother?"

"I believe you'll be on the lookout for a kindergarten teacher."

He half laughed. "I forgot I said that."

"I didn't."

"Ever thought about taking up early childhood education?"

A sad smile quivered about her lips. God, he loved that smile. Still holding her face, he leaned forward and tasted her lips. "Do you have any idea how much I need you?"

"Yes. I think I do."

"Because?" When she didn't answer he filled the silence, "You need me, too?" She nodded and his heart soared. "There's nothing we can't overcome together. Did you tell her about the baby?" he asked.

"No. I think that might be best for you to do. Alone."

"Coward," he teased.

"Craven."

"I had hoped we'd tell her together. But given what's happened today and what's still to happen, it's probably best if I tell her now." Gabe pulled his phone from his pocket, hit a programmed speed-dial number. "Dad, how soon can you get out to the island?" He overrode his father's objections. "Yes, it's important. More important than your game. I'm about to tell Mum that Chastity and I are having a baby." He smiled. "Call Julia, she'll get the helicopter." He frowned as his father spoke some more. "It's okay. I'm way ahead of you. You'll see when you get out there. But do me one favor. Give it ten minutes and then phone Mum." He eased the phone back into his pocket.

"Why did you tell him to go to the island?"

"To be with Mum."

"But—"

"Just trust me."

She nodded her acceptance. "What did he say about the baby?"

"He said I should marry you."

"No."

"Yes. I knew he would. He's old-fashioned like that. Besides, he was looking for the path of least resistance. He's on the seventeenth hole and wants to finish his game." He took both her hands between his. He couldn't seem to stop touching this woman. His woman. "Dad will like you. And you'll like him, too." He saw the doubt in her eyes. "You both play the piano and like Beethoven."

"That means nothing."

"It's a start. Besides, Dad's easy. Smile at him, tell him you're having his granddaughter and he'll be putty in your hands.

"Now for the big one." He looked at Chastity and winked then hit another button on his phone.

"Cynthia."

Chastity could hear his mother's voice as she launched straight into a tirade. "Mum!" He cut her off. "Chastity and I are having a baby." A shriek—and not of joy—came from Gabe's phone, then a rapid, shrill string of language. Chastity caught words like "dead to me," and "destroying our family." She turned away from him, walked a couple of slow, numb circuits of the ferry, then paused at the stern to stare at the foamy wake trailing behind the boat.

By the time she made her way back, Gabe was chatting with a group of smiling, nodding passengers. He saw her waiting at the bow and came to join her. He leaned back against the rail, looking perfectly calm as he watched her.

"The phone call didn't sound like it was going well."

"She's coming round. You have to trust me on this. She has both snobby and drama queen down to an art, but beneath it all she has a heart. And she'll love having a grandchild. Particularly a granddaughter. She's complained often enough about being surrounded by males in the family." He looked at her, his brown eyes serious. "It *will* be okay."

"I know it will be okay because it'll be your problem, not mine." He'd said he loved her, but it was a bittersweet admission because their love wasn't going to be enough. Not if it meant hurting others.

In the distance a helicopter headed for what looked like Sanctuary Island.

He took her hand and led her to sit in the white plastic chairs affixed to the deck. "Let's enjoy the trip." Two seagulls took up sentry positions on the rail at the front of the ferry.

How could she possibly enjoy it when her heart was breaking? Being with him like this was torture. She wanted the simple togetherness to go on forever to delay the moment of their parting, but she also wanted to get the pain over and done with.

By the time the ferry pulled away from the last wharf of its rounds, there were only a few passengers dotted about the boat. Some indoors, one or two out. Gabe left her side and went to the bridge to speak to the captain. He then made the rounds of the remaining passengers, pausing by each of them for a few words. Chastity shook her head. It was like he was campaigning for something. And by the look of their smiles and nods, he was winning them over. She looked away. Not her problem.

Gabe came back.

"I'll put you on the birth certificate." She needed to assure him of that before she began to distance herself from him. Perhaps she should go away somewhere. Somewhere with no phones, no Internet, almost like Sanctuary Island. She could have laughed. She needed to go somewhere she couldn't give in to the temptation to call him, to talk to him, or even to follow what he was doing in the business world. "I know that's all you really wanted."

He clasped her hands. "It was all I wanted at the start. It's not now. Now I want so very much more."

"And all I wanted was to convince you that I'm not a bad person. I'll be a good mother."

"I know you will. Which doesn't mean we won't sometimes have differing opinions about how to raise our children, but we'll work it out."

"Children?"

"I thought four, but if you only want one I guess that's fine, too."

"Gabe, have you lost your mind?"

"I'm not sure about my mind. I don't think I've lost it. My heart, on the other hand, I'm positive about. I've lost it completely."

She took a half step back from him. "I'm going to get off this boat and then it'll be best if we don't see each other for a while."

He closed the gap and she didn't have the strength to widen it again. Not yet. "What kind of marriage would it be if we didn't see a whole lot of each other? Certainly not the kind I'm hoping for."

One word had her mentally stumbling as confusion, hope and then reality coalesced. "Marriage? You have lost your mind. We're not getting married."

"That could complicate things."

"Ladies and gentlemen," a deep voice sounded over the speaker system, "this is your captain speaking. We'll be making a brief unscheduled stop at Sanctuary Island and then getting underway on the trip back to the mainland. I understand some of you will be disembarking here. For those continuing on the journey, our arrival will be fifteen minutes later than scheduled."

"What's going on?"

A smile twitched at Gabe's lips. As they began rounding the point into the bay, the helicopter again came in low overhead. Gabe's phone rang. "All set?" he asked. Apparently receiving a satisfactory answer, he pocketed the phone.

He dropped down onto one knee and grasped her left hand as he pulled something from his other pocket, keeping it hidden, clenched in his fist. "Will you marry me?"

Chastity tried to pull her hand free. "Get up."

"Not till you answer."

"Then, no."

"Why not?"

"I answered, now get up."

"You didn't say why."

"I just can't."

"Can't? Not don't want to?"

"It amounts to the same thing."

Finally he stood. "Not at all. Do you love me? And this time I want the truth."

"Yes. I love you." The smile that lit his face only hurt her more. "But sometimes that's not enough."

"It's enough. I want to spend my life with you."

"I don't fit in your world."

"You fit perfectly because you are my world."

Her breath caught in her throat. She wanted what

he was offering so desperately that it scared her. "Gabe, we can't."

"Will you wear my ring while you think about it?"

He was sliding one of the shells they'd collected for Sophie over her ring finger before she could even answer. He silenced her protests with his kiss. "So, this *can't,* is it really because of my mother?"

"No. Maybe."

"What if we get her blessing? Scratch that, what if we get her grudging consent? Will you at least consider it?"

"Yes." He didn't have a hope in hell. He hadn't been in the room with Cynthia. Hadn't seen the fear of losing a son, and the determination to prevent it, in her eyes. "I'd consider it."

Gabe smiled. Confident and triumphant. "She'll want to put the blame on you. Trapping me into this marriage. But if you won't do it without her consent, then the blame falls on her. So she's going to agree. And then she can blame you for making me miserable, for being a terrible mother, a bad example to our children. Although what she'd like best of all is to give her consent and for you to refuse me. It just depends on who you care about making happy. Cynthia or me. And yourself. Because we will be happy together."

"What about your father?"

"Dad's wholly on the side of an easy life. Which, incidentally, he's not going to get either way."

He kissed her again. "I do have a proper engagement ring for you, one that's been in the family for generations. Julia's bringing it out."

"That's not necessary."

"I thought it was. Out of curiosity, once we get my

mother's consent, how long do you think your *considering* will take?"

"I don't know," she said hesitantly, when all she wanted was for him to take her in his arms again. Because when she was in his arms, she could believe that it really all would work out for them. Because it didn't seem possible that it wouldn't.

"All right then. We'll just have a party today. A thinking-about-marrying-me celebration. Though really now I'd rather be alone with you. I think I'd have a pretty good chance at speeding up your consideration if it was just the two of us."

She frowned her confusion and with gentle hands on her shoulders he turned her. Beyond the sparkling blue of the bay, bathed in sunlight, a white marquee stood on the shore, pennants blowing in the breeze. A crowd of people, most of them holding champagne flutes, stood near the jetty, waiting.

Chastity looked from the marquee to Gabe and back again, suddenly picking out people she knew. "You didn't?"

He lifted a shoulder. "I always knew when I found the woman I loved I wouldn't want to wait, that I'd want to marry her that very day. But I'm not going to pressure you."

"This is what you call no pressure?"

"Chastity, we host functions all the time. It's not pressure. These people are going to enjoy themselves and have a party whether it's a marriage or a thinking-about-marriage celebration. It's not like they've been looking forward to it for months."

"You helicoptered them out?"

"Some. Chartered boats for others."

"All these people are here for you?"

"And you."

"How could there be anyone here for me?"

"The upside of Cynthia having you investigated, in case you never thought there could be one, is that the investigator could give Julia a list of your friends."

To one side, along the shoreline a young girl twirled, her white skirts spinning out around her before she stooped to pick up shells. "Is that Sophie?"

Gabe smiled. "Yes. I thought she'd make a beautiful flower girl. When the time comes."

The ferry moored and all of the passengers got off, calling their congratulations to Gabe and Chastity. "I invited them to stay. They all accepted," Gabe said by way of explanation. As the last passenger cleared the gangplank, Cynthia picked her way up, her heels entirely wrong for the grated surface. She made her way straight to them, heels now clicking purposefully on the decking.

"I don't want to interrupt," she said, "but I need to talk to Chastity for a minute. Alone."

Chastity's heart pounded against her ribs.

"You okay with that?" Gabe's eyes searched her face.

"Yes." She'd avoided Cynthia for long enough. Their discussion in the chalet, while far from amicable, had made her stop viewing Cynthia as someone to be frightened of and rather someone who was herself frightened. And grieving. Whatever happened she had to have some kind of relationship with this woman who would be a grandmother to her child. Gabe nodded. "Call out if you need reinforcements. Or rescuing." He looked pointedly at his mother. "Remember that I love this woman." He walked to the other side of the boat.

Cynthia fixed her with a gaze very much like her son's. "Gabe never rebelled like Tom did. Growing up, he was always such a good boy. He always did the right thing. And by the right thing, I guess I mean he did what we asked of him. But just occasionally he would get something in his head, something he really wanted, or wanted to do or didn't want to do. And then...then there was no way on earth I or anyone else could convince him otherwise."

Chastity waited.

"It appears he feels that way about you. About marrying you."

"I won't marry him without your consent."

"He told me that you wouldn't. I'm not sure whether that's very honorable or very cunning."

Chastity remained silent.

"Gabe would have me believe—honorable. And Gabe is a good judge of character. Usually. Look, Chastity, I don't really know you, but Gabe has...clarified some things. And I might have misjudged you. If you do decide to marry him today, or even if you don't, I want you to have this." From around her wrist she unclasped a diamond bracelet. "It was my grandmother's before me. It can be your something old. And if you want, someday you can pass it on to your daughter. My granddaughter." She held the bracelet out to her.

"I don't know what to say." Chastity hesitated. "Thank you."

Cynthia smiled. "Now pass me your wrist." She encircled the glinting bracelet around Chastity's wrist.

"I'm not easy to know. Or to like. I understand that." Cynthia took a long time fastening the clasp. Finally she lifted her eyes to Chastity's. "But please don't take Gabe or my granddaughter away from me."

Chastity did something she'd never imagined doing and put her arms around Cynthia. "I won't. I would never."

Cynthia hugged her back, a single fierce squeeze. "I'd withdraw my consent if you did."

"So you do consent?" Chastity pulled back to study the other woman's face.

"Yes." Cynthia lifted her chin and smiled. "And graciously, I hope. Not, as my son might have suggested, grudgingly. And now it's up to you."

Gabe's hand came to rest on her shoulder as she watched Cynthia walk away. "And now it's up to you," his deep voice sounded in her ear. "Will you marry me?"

She slid her arms around his waist, tilted her head up to look at his face, the face she loved, the man she loved. "Yes."

"I want you to take my name."

"I wouldn't have it any other way."

* * * * *

*Fan favorite Leslie Kelly is bringing her readers
a fantasy so scandalous, we're calling it
FORBIDDEN!*

*Look for
PLAY WITH ME
Available February 2010
from Harlequin® Blaze™.*

"Aren't you going to say 'Fly me' or at least 'Welcome
Aboard'?"

Amanda Bauer didn't. The softly muttered word that
actually came out of her mouth was a lot less welcoming. And had fewer letters. Four, to be exact.

The man shook his head and tsked. "Not exactly the
friendly skies. Haven't caught the spirit yet this morning?"

"Make one more airline-slogan crack and you'll be
walking to Chicago," she said.

He nodded once, then pushed his sunglasses onto
the top of his tousled hair. The move revealed blue eyes
that matched the sky above. And yeah. They were twin-
kling. Damn it.

"Understood. Just, uh, promise me you'll say
'Coffee, tea or me' at least once, okay? Please?"

Amanda tried to glare, but that twinkle sucked the an-
noyance right out of her. She could only draw in a slow
breath as he climbed into the plane. As she watched her
passenger disappear into the small jet, she had to
wonder about the trip she was about to take.

Coffee and tea they had, and he was welcome to them. But her? Well, she'd never even considered making a move on a customer before. Talk about unprofessional.

And yet…

Something inside her suddenly wanted to take a chance, to be a little outrageous.

How long since she had done indecent things—or decent ones, for that matter—with a sexy man? Not since before they'd thrown all their energies into expanding Clear-Blue Air, at the very least. She hadn't had time for a lunch date, much less the kind of lust-fest she'd enjoyed in her younger years. The kind that lasted for entire weekends and involved not leaving a bed except to grab the kind of sensuous food that could be smeared onto—and eaten off—someone else's hot, naked, sweat-tinged body.

She closed her eyes, her hand clenching tight on the railing. Her heart fluttered in her chest and she tried to make herself move. But she couldn't—not climbing up, but not backing away, either. Not physically, and not in her head.

Was she really considering this? God, she hadn't even looked at the stranger's left hand to make sure he was available. She had no idea if he was actually attracted to her or just an irrepressible flirt. Yet something inside was telling her to take a shot with this man.

It was crazy. Something she'd never considered. Yet right now, at this moment, she was definitely considering it. If he was available…could she do it? Seduce a stranger. Have an anonymous fling, like something out of a blue movie on late-night cable?

She didn't know. All she knew was that the flight to Chicago was a short one so she had to decide quickly. And as she put her foot on the bottom step and began to climb up, Amanda suddenly had to wonder if she was about to embark on the ride of her life.

HARLEQUIN® *Blaze*™

*It all started
with a few naughty books....*

As a member of the Red Tote Book Club,
Carol Snow has been studying works of
classic erotic literature...but Carol doesn't
believe in love...or marriage. It's going to take
another kind of classic—Charles Dickens's
A Christmas Carol—and a little otherworldly
persuasion to convince her to go after her
own sexily ever after.

Cuddle up with

Her Sexy Valentine

by STEPHANIE BOND

Available February 2010

---

red-hot reads

HARLEQUIN
Ambassadors

Want to share your passion for reading Harlequin® Books?

Become a Harlequin Ambassador!

Harlequin Ambassadors are a group of passionate and well-connected readers who are willing to share their joy of reading Harlequin® books with family and friends.

You'll be sent all the tools you need to spark great conversation, including free books!

All we ask is that you share the romance with your friends and family!

You'll also be invited to have a say in new book ideas and exchange opinions with women just like you!

To see if you qualify* to be a Harlequin Ambassador, please visit www.HarlequinAmbassadors.com.

*Please note that not everyone who applies to be a Harlequin Ambassador will qualify. For more information please visit www.HarlequinAmbassadors.com.

Thank you for your participation.

BAP09BPA

REQUEST YOUR FREE BOOKS!

2 FREE NOVELS
PLUS 2
FREE GIFTS!

Passionate, Powerful, Provocative!

SDES10